TO BE THERE WITH YOU

TO BE THERE WITH YOU

Gayla Reid

[signature: Gayla Reid]

Douglas & McIntyre

VANCOUVER / TORONTO

Douglas & McIntyre
1615 Venables Street
Vancouver, British Columbia
V5L 2H1

Canadian Cataloguing in Publication Data

Reid, Gayla.
To be there with you

ISBN 1-55054-176-5

I. Title.
PS8585.E42T6 1994   C813'.54   C94-910527-9
PR9199.3.R44T6 1994

All characters in *To Be There with You* are entirely fictional.
Any resemblance they may bear to real persons and
experiences is illusory.

Excerpt from *Around the Boree Log* by John O'Brien appears
with the permission of Angus and Robertson/HarperCollins
Publishers Australia.

The publisher gratefully acknowledges the assistance of the
Canada Council and the British Columbia Ministry of
Tourism, Small Business, and Culture for its publishing
programs.

Editing by Barbara Pulling
Cover illustration by Luc Melanson
Cover and text design by Michael Solomon
Typeset by Compeer Typographic Services Ltd.
Printed and bound in Canada by Metropole Litho
Printed on acid-free paper ♾

In memory of my parents,
Mabel & Jim Reid

ACKNOWLEDGEMENTS

When I began writing in my forties I found that despite decades as an editor and a student of literature, I experienced all the hopes and fears of the novice writer. These are, I suspect, even more intense for those of us who get off to a late start.

For this reason, I am especially appreciative of the timely encouragement and generous support I have received. I owe a particular debt of gratitude to: McClelland & Stewart, for the Journey Prize; CBC Radio and *Saturday Night*, for the Short Story Literary Award; the National Magazine Awards Foundation; Douglas Glover of *Coming Attractions*, and the editors at *Prism international*.

And in a category all of her own, I want to thank Eleanor Wachtel—for everything.

Some of these stories have appeared in slightly different form in the following journals and anthologies: *Saturday Night, The Malahat Review, Prism international, The Capilano Review, Prairie Fire, Island Magazine, The Journey Prize Anthology 1993, Coming Attractions 1993* and *Frictions II.*

CONTENTS

Sister Doyle's Men

IN this photograph my mother is on horseback. Behind her, there is a row of hills. Gums are tossing in the wind. (They look like gums, anyway.) The horse has its head turned sharply. I suspect she is holding the reins too tightly.

This is, as my mother's handwriting on the back of the picture says, "somewhere in New Guinea."

At one corner of the photograph you can see the shadow of the person who is holding the camera. You can make out the shape of the hat. It's a slouch hat, pinned up on one side.

"Who's that?" I ask my mother, pointing to the shadow.

There is a slight pause. Then she says, "One of the men."

My mother is wearing trousers and a shirt. It is wartime.

My mother grew up in Sydney's eastern suburbs. "Where on earth did you learn to ride?" I ask her.

"You learned," she says. "You learned fast. All sorts of things."

It is a black-and-white photo, of course, but the contrast is sharp. "The hills look very green," I say.

My mother looks at the photo again. "I was green all right," she says. She laughs. "You can say that again. I'd only been there three and a half months when that was taken."

I wondered why she mentioned the months, and so precisely.

My mother was a sergeant in the AAMWS, the women's wing of the Australian Army Medical Service.

My father was in the Seventh Division. My father was a Rat at Tobruk. When Australia's Prime Minister Curtin brought the Seventh home my father was promptly sent to New Guinea, where he was involved in the fighting around Kokoda.

My father told no war stories, kept no war souvenirs. (Unless, as my brother says, you want to count Mum.) But my mother spoke of the war often, which, given her work, was not surprising.

"He brought them home," she'd say, of Curtin. "He was determined that Australia would not go. He gave those poms what for, he did."

When I was a child I thought everybody knew about the Seventh, how the prime minister brought them home.

My mother met my father in Moresby. They got married right away. Six months later, I was born.

As adolescents, my brother and I consider this story. I am horrified. (What if the nuns find out?) My brother, on the other hand, is much impressed. "The sly old goat," he says. "You've got to give it to him."

"What was she like when you first met?" I ask my father.

He says the usual things: good looker, always one for a laugh. "No," I say, "what was she like, really?"

I should know better.

"Oh, things were at sixes and sevens, in those days," my father says. My father is one of those old-style Australians who guards his personal life with a wildly unwarranted tenacity. My father gives nothing away. My mother's secrets are safe with him.

Why did she choose my father? My brother and I decided it was because he had come through unscathed. Both in the Middle East and in New Guinea my father was what he calls one lucky bastard. My mother knew she was going to need one undamaged man in her life.

For somewhere in the green hills of New Guinea, my mother became acquainted with death. Despite her seamless, unspoiled husband, despite the clamour of her two children, she did not return to the house of the living, not completely.

My mother was Sister Doyle.

Sister Doyle was in charge of the ward in Rhodes Repat. where they kept the men who had been wounded in the war and who would never recover. Those men, still breathing but in essential ways already dead, were her life.

For a child in my mother's house, certain appearances on that ward are mandatory.

There is the Christmas party, held in mid-December. We sing away in a manger, no crib for a bed. We pass out gifts: magazines, books, lollies, cigarettes. These last for those who still have lips with which to suck, to smoke.

There is the afternoon of Christmas Day itself. We go from bed to bed with trays of fruitcake, with glasses of port and Scotch with straws in them. We take our presents to show the men.

We are not the only children summoned to Sister Doyle's ward. Her men are to have music, the sounds of children, singing.

The Catholic kids sing "God Bless Our Lovely Morning Land." The state school kids sing "Old King Cole" and (in possibly dubious taste) "I Am a Happy Wanderer." The choirs do not go right into the ward, as we do. They stand at the milder end. If they are lucky they do not even notice the odd small lumps further down the ward. They do not see the beds at the far end.

These beds have mysterious hoops in places where faces usually are.

Adults come, too, to entertain. On New Year's Eve the local pipe band comes to pipe out the old and in the new. They march up and down the ward, these pipers. But they are grown up. They know when and where not to look.

The scoutmaster comes to our house with money from the bottle drive.

"That will go towards a very fine Easter hamper, and I know you know how much it means to the men," my mother tells him, appreciative. He blushes.

They all come—the Rotary blokes, the Lions, the Masons, the St. Vincent de Paul—my mother makes no sectarian distinctions. This is the early fifties and they wear the little Returned Services League badges in their lapels.

They are, all of them, returned men.

I learned that phrase naturally, without thinking. Later it seemed to typify the to-hell-and-back theme—which had great currency at that time. For the men on the ward, who did not really return, it seemed especially fraught.

When my mother sits with the returned men in the lounge room, they tell war stories. These stories are exceptionally vague, innocent, featureless.

Here's one: There was this anti-aircraft gunner in Darwin. Name of Bluey. Anyhow, Bluey, he had this sulphur-crested cockatoo. When the air-raid siren went, the cocky said: "Time to get under the sink, Blue."

I did not understand why they found this amusing. But how they laughed.

Conversation grows a little more interesting when there are other nurses there. They talk about the tents they used as operating theatres. "Oh, the mud," my mother says. "Oh, the stench," the other nurses say, happily.

If I were asked to construct a portrait of somebody in my mother's position at that time, I would certainly make her a monarchist, a believer in religion, and a conservative in politics. But my mother was, curiously, none of these things.

She saw religion as having its uses, however. She favoured Anglican funerals. "They give the best sendoff," she said. "The flowers of the field."

Her interest in politics cut off at 1945. She was not in any sense a cold-war warrior and in that embodiment of fifties stodge, Australia's Prime Minister Menzies, took no interest one way or another. The fifties, for my mother, meant Korea. And Korea meant two new men on the ward. My mother worried they wouldn't fit in. They were younger.

As a young adult I would say that my mother was, at heart, the universal soldier. (And she really was to blame.)

There was this man on the ward, Teddy. He'd been in my father's unit. Came from the bush, out Walgett way. Used to ride in all the shows before the war, my father said. A crack shot, too, was Teddy.

That was how my father met my mother—Stan had gone to the hospital in Moresby, looking for his mate Teddy.

Teddy could not move. His spine was a write-off. He couldn't speak, either. He could move his eyes from side to side and that was about it. Teddy got totally messed up in New Guinea. Over the years Teddy improved, gradually, until he could manage to talk a little. To the outside it was just gobble-gobble, but Sister Doyle could decipher every word.

This is what Teddy said: "I'm in this and I'm doing the best I can."

When my mother liked someone, when she considered them to be her friend, she'd tell them about Teddy. When she repeated what Teddy said, she never used the third person. She always adopted the first person: "I'm in this and I'm doing the best I can."

"How's Teddy?" my father would ask my mother.

"He's a battler, is Teddy," my mother would say. And her voice would be full of something heavy, like love.

I think now of how Stan met her when he went to Moresby.

She walked down the corridor towards him, listening to the floorboards creak, her stomach in a knot. (Outside, through the louvres, the green hills.)

He figured it out soon enough, he realized how things stood with her. And his face barely moved a muscle.

That would have reassured my mother, she would have decided then.

On Christmas Day, when I am eight, this happens:

We are in the ward, and I am sitting at a window. It is a quarter to five, the end of the afternoon.

Earlier, we were all here, my father and brother as well. My brother got a cocker spaniel puppy for Christmas, named Queenie—this is the Coronation year. A boy should have a dog, my mother says. Queenie was brought in to show the men.

My father has taken Queenie and my brother home. My father and my brother are already besotted with Queenie. They take turns carrying her with excited tenderness.

The men, those who could reach out, felt Queenie's soft round head, stroked her ears. Those who could see looked into her brown eyes. Queenie was a big success.

Around afternoon-tea time there was a full-blown high summer thunderstorm. (My mother hurried to the men who whimpered.) Then the furious rain. Now it is over, and the ward is filled with a peculiar golden light. My mother has thrown open the windows and the smell of rain rinsing through the hot earth, the smell of fallen gum leaves fragrantly rotting, fills the room.

My mother is sitting on a chair between two of the beds, and everything is calm. She has brought her men through the fracturing demands of Christmas Day, with its forced cheer. She has given them her children, and Queenie. She has stood by them in the thunderstorm, and now she has for them this coolness, this relief.

I look at my mother, and with a piercing clarity I see how she is resolute and obsessed. And I am her daughter. *As she is, so I will become.* I am suffused with this fact; I am magnified —not by joy but by a terrible certitude. And I am really very frightened.

I look away from my mother. I inspect my presents from the other nurses. My favourite is a wooden pencil box. It has two storeys. You swing out part of the top layer and there is a secret second layer, beneath. I slide my finger into the farthest recesses of the pencil box, in that second layer, beneath the place for the rubber. I plan what I will put there.

It is so quiet I can hear the clock ticking at the end of the ward, near the entrance. Instead of numbers it has the words, *Lest We Forget.* The small hand is on the second *E,* the big hand has just passed the *G.*

My mother was always so busy that it took me a long time to realize what her main burden was: the slow grinding of time, its absolute refusal to pass.

Sister Doyle knows all their birthdays. A good six weeks before the birthday of Shorty or Curly or Jacko (they keep their boyish wartime nicknames) my mother writes to his family. In recalcitrant cases, she telephones. Trunks please, she asks, her voice serious. I wish to place a trunk call.

As you know, she says, when the call goes through, Shorty/Curly/Jacko has his birthday coming up. Can we be expecting a parcel? As you know, he's quite fond of Capstans/Winning Post Chocolates/Pix or Post. And it has been some time, let me see, three years, hasn't it? I'd just like to let you know how very welcome you'd be, if it were possible. At all possible.

The parcels arrive—from Dubbo, from Grafton, from Condobolin—drawn by the strength of my mother's will. Sometimes the people come, too.

Apart from the holidays, Christmas, New Year, Easter, there is—of course—the big day itself, the one day of the year: Anzac Day.

My mother knows which division each of her men was in. She has the ward decorated with the appropriate emblems and colours and mascots. Radios are laid on, and, in later years, television sets. Nobody is to miss out on the dawn service and the march. In the afternoon, there is rum and Bonox.

So they inch forward, Sister Doyle's men.

At the end of the road, there is the funeral. And if only a handful of inattentive relatives can be rounded up (thank God that's over), there is the inexpensive solemnity of the last post. And there is, from the priest or minister, these words: They gave their lives. For that public gift they received a praise which never ages and a tomb most glorious—not so much the tomb in which they lie, but that in which their fame survives, to be remembered forever, when occasion comes for word or deed.

I'm not sure where that comes from. It's something I absorbed from my mother, much as other daughters learn to sew a frock or cook a cake.

My mother is never completely off duty. We are walking down to Central to catch the train. My mother points out to us—

my brother and me—the plaque on the overpass at the Chalmers Street end: *Past this point marched THE MEN WHO WENT.* In Martin Place, at the cenotaph, we are not permitted to giggle and fool around. If there are wreaths—and there often are—we are to read them quietly, and with respect.

At school I learn how the Spartans put their children out to die. That reminds me of my mother. If we disgraced her on the ward, I tell my brother, she would put us out to die.

She would be capable of it.

I am making my mother seem formidable. She was that, indeed. But in many ways she was a permissive parent.

My brother and I are allowed to have comics, and she never checks to see if we are doing our homework. A lot of the time she isn't there. She's at work. It is my father who is nominally in charge.

My father, the unscathed survivor, came home from the war and got a job as a clerk at the lotteries office. At five sharp he takes the train home and retreats to his shed. In the shed he keeps all his carpentry tools, his workbench and his radio. He also has two old lounge chairs (it's a good-sized shed). In one of these chairs he sits and smokes his pipe. The other one is for Queenie, and us kids when we come to watch.

My father builds things.

In the fifties my father undertakes two projects that see him through the decade. First, he puts a second storey on the house. This is a posh, unusual thing to do in the ordinary Sydney suburb of West Ryde. Then he builds a whole bunch of built-in furniture. Built-in furniture, in highly lacquered wood, is the very latest thing.

My brother and I each acquire rooms of our own on the top floor, with windows that look out on the jacaranda. In my bedroom my father builds a dressing table that has a bookcase in one side. I can put my hand out and select a book without even getting out of bed.

In the kitchen he constructs a breakfast nook: a round pink Laminex table, with a high banquette, just like in a restaurant.

But his tour de force is in the lounge room. There a combined china cabinet-sideboard-radiogram dominates one wall, a triumph in blond wood.

It is an extraordinary home. It could look like something out of *House and Gardens*, only my mother doesn't complete the effect. In my bedroom I have some secondhand curtains she picked up at the hospital fete.

My brother's friends love the house. Not for its furniture, but because it is always in turmoil. Constantly, one room or another is uninhabitable, owing to the construction work.

My mother is not in the least put out by this. Quite the contrary. "We'll just have to make do," she declares, and her voice is girlish and gay.

The kitchen is a mess and my brother's friends are staying to tea. My mother takes the toaster into the lounge room. We have toast and sardines and listen to "Pick-a-Box."

"The money or the box?" asks Bob Dyer.

"The box, the box," the boys shout, their eyes shining, eager for whatever life will throw at them.

They are always around, the visiting boys. There is the marvellous chaos and, what's more, the place is reliably provisioned. My mother goes to cakeshops and buys lamingtons, sponges, biscuits.

This is a shady thing to do, in the fifties — store-bought cakes are looked down upon. "I simply don't have time," my mother says, firmly.

My brother's friends help themselves to the rest of the lamingtons and watch my father working. When they've eaten those they can get some Minties from the shed. My father keeps boxes of Minties down there. Minties have cartoons on the side of the box: a fisherman has just reeled in a pair of ladies' corsets.

I don't get in the boys' way (they're just little kids, really, so boring). I'm upstairs, staring out at the jacaranda, which is on fire with purple flowers.

I'm reading books about girls' schools with no nuns.

I'm looking in the women's magazines, examining the Meds ads. No belts, no pads, no pins. No odour.

My father, Stan Doyle, had been brought up in a Catholic orphanage. He had left school after sixth class and had learned, as my mother put it, "to turn his hand to anything." Had we lived in the bush, Stan would have turned his hand to sheep and cattle. In the desert, he'd have known exactly where to find water.

That a man of manifold skills was putting in his days at the lotteries office was never remarked upon.

After the orphanage, Stan was caught up in the Depression, and after the Depression he went to the war. Yet Stan is a calm man, sweet and peaceable. A man to turn to in time of crisis.

My mother had to sign papers to say she'd have the kids brought up Catholic. And sign she did.

Off I went to the nuns. When it comes time for my brother to go to school, my mother puts her foot down. He could go for religious instruction. He could make his first communion and all that baloney. But he was to attend the state school and get a real education.

"The nuns are good enough for girls but they won't do for boys," my mother says.

Stan doesn't argue. He isn't an arguing man. But it makes him nervous, I can tell.

Without ever putting it in words, Stan lets me know precisely what he thinks of nuns and priests: a dangerous, slightly looney lot, but powerful. Best to keep on their good side.

Hard lessons, from his own childhood.

At Sunday mass, my father sidles in just before the end of the sermon and sits, ill at ease, near the door—poised for easy and early escape. He looks exactly like one of those kids that sit at the back of the classroom.

I am the only one in my class who comes from a "mixed marriage." The nuns know.

Whose family isn't saying the daily rosary?

I have to put up my hand.

On the way home from school we exchange insults with the state school kids.

Catholics, Catholics
eat snails and frogs.

We reply with the more esoteric:

Proddies, Proddies
fall off logs.

In this way I learn that one side needs the other, even for the completion of a rhyme.

Sometimes in these roaming bands of state school kids I see my brother's friends. My brother himself.

I wait for the question: "Isn't that your *brother*?"

We are driving over to my aunt's house. We are in the Holden. As we approach the house we can see all the cars, already lined up.

"The football team's out in force," says my mother, signalling disapproval. Her sister's husband comes from a vast family. They dominate these gatherings with a beery, self-congratulatory clannishness.

My aunt, unlike my mother, leads an ordinary life. She stays home. She makes elaborate desserts: rice pudding and jelly layered in tall clear glasses.

I wish my mother would learn to do things like that.

"How's the house going?" my aunt asks my father. He is a fool, her tone proclaims, to squander all that upon my mother, who has not eyes with which to see.

"Stan's got a real showplace," my aunt tells one of the football team. "It could be a real showplace, you know," she says to my mother. (If only you were prepared to pull your weight.)

"Humm," says my mother, bored. "What a delicious dessert. I don't know how you do it. Really I don't."

But when we drive home my mother is in a good mood. The visit to the relatives is behind her, one more time. "That wasn't too bad," she says. "Wasn't too bad, Stan, was it?" She's stuck it out and now it's over. She can get on with things. She can get back to the ward.

I look out the window of the Holden and see our ridiculous, extravagant house poking up above all the others. I know we are not a normal family.

We are weird.

My father, who had no childhood family, isn't much of a patriarch. You could say he never developed the knack. But we learn from him, my brother and I. We sit in the old lounge chair in the shed, chewing on Minties and playing with Queenie and, without even know what we are doing, find out how to use a padsaw, a mitre box.

With my father, I have no quarrel.

It's a different story when it comes to my mother. There are scenes.

In this particular scene we are fighting, my mother and me. We are shouting at each other, we are choking out sobs and insults. We are in an uproar.

Just as Anzac Day is a big day on the ward, it is a big day in our family life. Each year, my father gets out his medals and goes to the march. Each year, my brother and I go with him, to watch and wave and pick him out and feel important. At the end of the march, a photographer takes our picture: my father, my brother and me, standing together in Martin Place. In early years, there were always street photographers on hand. In later years my father takes his own camera and asks one of his mates to "do the honours." When the picture is developed, it stands on the mantleshelf in the lounge room, where it stays until the new one takes its place.

In this way (I wrote in my diary) our lives are measured out in Anzac Days (three exclamation marks).

This year I'm refusing to go.

I've been to see the play *The One Day of the Year*. This play —which was, I am convinced, written especially with me in mind—portrays a young man who exposes our celebrations, our observances.

Anzac Day turns out to be so much drunken jingoism.

I came out of the Palace Theatre and vomited into a rubbish bin.

So I won't go to the march, and what's more . . .

"This place is a madhouse," I tell my mother. "You've been ramming it down our throats all our lives. It's crazy. It's sick. I have a life to get on with, in case you haven't noticed."

"The war happened," my mother says, sharply.

"You could at least stop glorifying the bloody thing," I return.

"I do not," she declares, offended to her soul, "I do not *glorify* anything."

"You do, you do," I reply, going for the upper registers. "You do, you rub our noses in it."

"I do not glorify anything," she repeats (I have really scored, there). "Except courage, courage in the face of pain and loss and despair."

This is as close as I ever come to hearing my mother's apologia for her work.

I flee to the shed, to enlist my father's support.

"You have to stop her," I inform him. "Show her."

He is quiet and mild and he exasperates the hell out of me. "Show her what?" he asks, refusing to be drawn in.

"You're both hopeless," I shout. "The pair of you."

About this time my mother has a big row with my brother, too. About Teddy.

My brother and I joke about Teddy, but most secretly. It is utter blasphemy. My brother is keen on gymnastics and practises every evening. He stands on his head and he says, for our mutual pleasure: "I'm in this and I'm doing the best I can."

We laugh and he tries his best to keep from toppling over.

My mother catches him at it. She chases him through the house, trying to grab him and hit him. He speeds out onto the road and my mother—to my surprise—does not pursue him. Instead she sits down in the breakfast nook and begins to cry, in a hoarse, windy kind of way.

"You kids don't care about anyone except yourselves, do you," she says. In her voice I hear the beginning of an appeal. I leave the room in a hurry.

Eventually my brother creeps back into the house. For about three weeks my mother treats him as if he doesn't exist.

My brother and I hold whispered, mutinous meetings in my room. We brim with righteous solidarity.

"She should never have taken us to the ward when we were just little kids," I say. "Doesn't she realize we were *scared*?"

"Dad's just as bad," my brother says.

"He just lets her rip," I agree.

Even as we speak we can hear him. He is hammering away on the stairs, replacing a baluster.

One day my mother comes home early from work. This is a shocking thing, without precedent. I'm at home because it's a big feast day — the Feast of the Assumption — and the nuns have given us the day off.

The nuns are always giving us the day off, or so my brother says. It's a wonder you ever learn anything, he says.

I go downstairs to find out what's going on. Is she sick?

She takes her hat off and puts it on the kitchen table.

"Teddy's gone," she says. "Teddy. He begged for it," she says. "For ages and ages. Nothing else. Just that. After all these years. I had to give him what he wanted, you know. I had to." Her voice sounds automatic. (Does she know who she's speaking to? Does she even know she's speaking?)

She takes a chair and goes outside to the back patio that my father built a few years ago. She's still got her overcoat on. It is the kind of grey, still day you get once or twice in Sydney during August. A low day.

She's still there at a quarter to six when my father gets home. He takes her a rug and a cup of tea. She pushes away the rug and ignores the tea.

She sits out there in the dark.

My father goes out again, this time to persuade her to come in. I can see him talking to her and I can see her not even turning her head.

He comes back in and he's got a funny kind of embarrassed look on his face, as if he's been caught doing something foolish.

"Let's have beans on toast, eh?" he says.

I make the toast, my brother puts the jug on. My father lights the gas and gets the beans going. We huddle together in the breakfast nook; the three of us, and Queenie.

At last she does come in. My brother and I are in my room. We are supposed to be asleep by this time. She goes up the stairs and into their bedroom. My brother and I creep along the hallway and listen for voices.

Nothing.

What did he say to her?

What did she, finally, say to him?

It is the late sixties and my mother has cancer. She is in Rhodes Repat., so she is, in her own way, at home.

They are fooling about trying to decide which parts of her to cut out. "I've told them to get on with it," my mother says. "Chop, chop." My mother has a nurse's cheery crudity about such things.

Now, of all times, she isn't going to let her men down. She calls for a wheelchair. "They've seen tons of people in their dressing gowns," she says. "Might as well see me."

Off she goes to the ward. I wonder if it distresses the men, to have her growing thinner and more determined by the day.

By this time there is another war, about which I have come to hold passionate views. It has given me a glimpse of what my life might be, what I might become.

My days and nights are full of organizing against the war. Our country's involvement in this war has to end, the war itself has to end. So many other things have to change, and fundamentally. There is everything to be done. I go about in a state of euphoric fatigue.

These visits to the hospital are really very difficult to fit in. It takes two bus rides and a change of trains just to get here. And I have vital work to do.

In my mother's presence I scrupulously avoid all mention of the war.

She's the one who brings it up.

"I was reading in the *Herald*," she says, "they can bring boys home now that they wouldn't have been able to before." She says this in a puzzled voice. "They can get them out so quickly, and the know-how is so much better."

How can the Vietnam boys (the MEN WHO WENT) be worse off than the men on the ward and still be alive?

She looks at me—to me—for an answer.

My brother has been conscripted but has disappeared into Western Australia instead. Wisely, he does not write.

Officials knock on the door. Plainclothes men, and on one occasion the military police. They come to the house. They come to my flat in Bondi.

With my father they are polite. With me, contemptuous, hostile.

No, he's not here. No, I'm not expecting him. No, I don't know where he is. No, no, no.

When my mother is dying, when she is rambling, out of it on morphine, and there is no more question of her ever getting up and going anywhere, she calls out their names: Curly, Joey, Teddy, Blue, Jacko, Stan, Teddy, Shorty, Rusty, Teddy.

With the endless need of the child, I listen for my name, and for my brother's. She does not call them.

My father is left alone in the big empty house.

These days Stan lives with my brother. When I go back to Australia, I stay with them.

My brother, who runs an orchard on the Murrumbidgee, has an old-fashioned home with big verandahs. At the weekends the place is often filled with friends (the visiting boys).

At the back of the house Stan built what he calls a grandpa flat. There's a small workshop down there. Although he is now in his eighties, he is making for my brother a desk out of stunning dark Tasmanian sassafras.

"Lovely, lovely," my brother says, stroking the wood with his hand and looking in his father's face.

"It'll see me out," Stan says, of the grandpa flat.

My brother writes to me, he keeps me up to date.

We were sorting through some old snaps the other day — my brother wrote — and we came across a really early one of Mum, in her nurse's uniform, on what looked like a troopship.

Both arms around some strange young man, a soldier. And smiling. Smiling to beat the band.

"Where did that one come from?" my brother asks Stan. "I don't remember ever seeing that one before."

"Oh, that'd be Teddy's," Stan says, easily. "Used to carry it everywhere with him."

"Teddy's?" says my brother.

"Teddy's," Stan says.

"Used to *carry* it everywhere with him?" my brother says.

"That'd be right, I reckon," Stan says slowly, evasive now. "Before. Before he. You know. Got messed up."

Then — my brother wrote — the old coot gets up and pours himself a cup of tea. Stares off into the middle distance, as if bored.

When I come home they drive up to Sydney to meet me: Stan, my brother and his wife.

We go to visit my mother's grave.

She has a small bronze plaque. The rising sun of the Australian Infantry Forces is in the top right-hand corner.

I put my arm through Stan's. I look over at my brother.

Stan looks down at the grave, at Sister Doyle's name.

I don't say anything.

Stan lifts his bony face, sniffing the air. He turns to my brother.

He says: "When I get completely buggered I'll go down the back paddock and you can shoot me."

"Oh, Dad," says my brother's wife. "You mustn't talk like that, not when we love you so. It isn't right."

Passport

1

In 1958, this is what Marion knew about Budapest:

Cardinal Mindszenty.

Sister Agnes had told them about Cardinal Mindszenty. He had been imprisoned by the Communists. He had been tortured but he had not given in.

The freedom fighters. Crushed by Russian tanks.

Marion had heard about their final messages to the world.

Help, help, help. S O S, S O S, S O S. Now I have to run over to the next room to fire some shots.

We shall die for Hungary.

They were devout Catholics, all of them, Sister Agnes said.

They were fighting godless atheistic Communism with their bare hands. For a few days, they had won.

We have wounded who have given their blood for the sacred cause of liberty, but we have no medicine. The last piece of bread has been eaten.

Sacred liberty, betrayal, martyrdom. Such things (Marion knew) were not possible in Australia.

There was Reverend Mother at the front of the classroom, come to introduce Magda Szanto, from Budapest. With her shining red hair.

Marion thought competition for her would be fierce.

But the class was, at that time, preoccupied with other matters. If you drank Coca-Cola at lunchtime and put blotting paper in your shoes you'd be drunk by midafternoon.

It's working, they shrieked, giggling with fervour.

Magda, who at home drank a glass of wine and was permitted a little of the fiery *barack*, stared.

They took their revenge.

Smells funny, they said.

A DP.

A reffo.

Garlic on her breath.

So it was Marion who walked home, unimpeded, beside Magda. Marion who met Magda's mother.

Magda's mother served little cakes with dark nuts in the middle, and looked at Marion while she ate them.

Marion's mouth went dry.

It was Marion who sat with Magda and Magda's mother in front of their first television set. On Saturday nights, Marion explained "Leave It to Beaver" and "77 Sunset Strip."

In Magda's house Marion found herself, for the first time, an expert. She leaned back; she stretched her arms out along the sofa.

Have some more cakes, Magda's mother said to her.

Thank you very much, Marion said, behaving nicely. Really very tasty. She smiled at Magda's mother.

Warily, Magda's mother smiled back.

Magda's father was an engineer, down at the Snowy, and seldom home. (He had a most peculiar name: Bandi, a fact Marion knew she must, for her own sake, conceal from the other girls.)

Marion's father was buried at Waverley, along with her grandparents and great-grandparents. The whole shooting match, Marion explained, to Magda.

Magda had other cemeteries from other shooting matches. Kerepes Cemetery in Pest, for one.

Her brother Laszlo was buried there.

After the second invasion, Magda told Marion, they took the freedom fighters and hanged them on the bridges, in clusters.

Like bunches of winter grapes, Magda said.

They walked out at night, across the swamp. They were twelve hours in the swamp.

And at last they were in a hut on the far side. It was cold in the hut. (It was cold everywhere.) A bare light bulb overhead.

Magda was sleepy, sleepy.

Behind her somewhere, men were talking in low, urgent voices.

Her mother took her handkerchief, wet it with saliva and tried to clean Magda's face with it.

Furious, Magda pushed her mother away.

Magda showed Marion the pictures of the freedom fighters, from the newspapers.

The freedom fighters were dressed in funny old clothes.

They looked, in particular, at a girl in a beret. This girl had a big bandage on her cheek and was immensely serious.

She was their own age. There was no doubt about it.

Just think, Magda told Marion. Think of what I could have done.

I could have saved Laszlo.

2

Even in the classroom, built in double brick to last as long as faith, it's hot and moist. Out in the garden cicadas are shouting all the way to the convent walls.

Beyond the walls lies the city. Where tar is melting in the streets and flies are forcing their way in. Where good Catholic girls like Marion and Magda are going to be exposed to non-Catholics of a lower moral standard.

Today is the end of year one-day retreat for the fourth and fifth years. Not to be confused with the big one, the three-day retreat, in the middle of winter. This is just a final tune-up before the summer holidays.

In the morning, there is mass and confession in the chapel. In the afternoon, it's back to the classroom for the annual lecture on chastity.

The purpose of chastity, the Jesuit says, and writes it on the blackboard, is to control sex attraction. There are two kinds of sex attraction, he says, making two arrows with his chalk: personal sex attraction and physical sex attraction.

Personal sex attraction, says the Jesuit, turning boldly to face them, is the fascination a person can have for a person of the opposite sex.

In the realm of personal sex attraction, he says, a young Catholic girl has a special example to follow, the example of the Blessed Virgin Mary. For immodest dress in girls provides an occasion of sin to boys.

The serge of her tunic sticks to Marion's thighs. The day is as moist as.

The priest clears his throat and says: For boys have passions that are more easily aroused.

The silence in the room is enormous. It billows out into the garden where the cicadas, abruptly, halt.

Marion is falling from the chapel tower, just like Kim Novak in *Vertigo*. Falling is dangerous and lovely and quiet. Kim Novak's eyes are an incitement to sins against chastity, surely? (For boys, who have passions that are more easily aroused.)

Physical sex attraction, the priest writes next. Outside marriage, he says—turning very swiftly—this is a mortal sin. He turns back to the board, writes Outside Marriage, and underlines it three times.

It is a mortal sin to enjoy or to desire any sexual pleasure outside marriage, he repeats, tapping at the underlining with his chalk. Whether prolonged or momentary.

(Marion and Magda were in Magda's mother's room, with the blinds down, trying on Magda's mother's underwear. Magda had on her mother's best petticoat, apricot lace and something silky. The soft smell of powder on Magda's skin. Was that prolonged or momentary?)

The priest has fine white hands, with small black hairs growing along his fingers. Sacred fingers, that have touched the host. Never touching himself. No, he never.

For any unmarried person any full consent to venereal pleasure, alone or with others, is a mortal sin.

Marion has seen the word in public lavatories, on little notices made out of tin and painted with enamel.

Venereal. Disease.

Venereal, he says, from the Roman goddess Venus. Meaning pleasure that is achieved by movement in the sexual parts of the body.

In the garden Sister Agnes is tying up the agapanthus. Sister Agnes was in Thailand last year, and came back looking yellow.

In Thailand, Sister Agnes said, one can smell the devil.

Agapanthus, Agatha's pants. Huge blue blooms that signal the start of summer.

Agape, love. Anthos, a flower. Will thrive even if neglected. Her father had told her.

Afterwards, Marion and Magda walk home together, as usual. Magda kicks at the footpath. Magda tells Marion this:

Her brother, Laszlo, had a girlfriend, a lover. She had been killed in a big demonstration in Parliament Square, one October Thursday early in the fighting.

A *lover*. It was—European.

Magda said, angrily: Were they mortal sinners? Have they gone to hell?

I don't think so, Marion said, to comfort. Although it followed, they would have gone to hell, wouldn't they? The priest had just spent all afternoon telling them.

What if she said something and Magda went, what? what?

Magda has Laszlo, she has history. (*We shall die for Hungary.*)

Marion walks along beside Magda.

On the other side of the world, Laszlo is in a dark room in Budapest. He stands at the window. His lover, behind him on the bed, is wearing nothing but her petticoat.

It is unimaginable, venereal.

Russian tanks clank through the streets.

3

It was Magda who did brilliantly in the Leaving Certificate. Marion didn't do as well as everyone expected.

It's not worth going back and doing it all over again, her mother said.

Money doesn't grow on trees, her mother said. Who's to say you'd do any better next time round?

No, Marion was to do a secretarial course at the Tech.

Then that nice Gerry Connolly had agreed to take her on.

Gerry Connolly was a man who came to their house to say the family rosary. The rosary, which had been top of the charts all the way through the fifties, was by now somewhat out of fashion. But those who valued the Blessed Virgin Mary weren't going to let themselves be put off by young fools in Rome who were rushing around throwing open doors and windows.

Gerry Connolly and the others had a blessed statue of Our Lady of Fatima, which they took from house to house. They gathered around it and contemplated the joyful, sorrowful and glorious mysteries.

Marion took the bus and went to type things for Gerry Connolly. On his desk, Gerry had a big picture of the family: Gerry and Theresa and the kids—Bernadette, Damien, Aloysius, Kevin, Dominic, Ignatius, and the twins, Gerard and Paul.

Magda went to Sydney University. She dressed all in black and she wore white lipstick.

Marion got a black sweater herself and wore it to the uni with Magda. They sat in the student union and Magda pointed out important people to her.

They went up to the Cross and drank Chianti with their spaghetti bolognese. Marion giggled at the prostitutes. Magda frowned.

Marion had her own room at home. I'm not one to pry, her mother said, but really she should be keeping the place looking tidy. There was nothing to stop her, nothing at all, from going to the dances the Young Catholic Workers put on. On Saturday afternoons, after she'd helped her mother with the housework, she could have a shower and put on a pretty frock.

On Sundays at St. Kevin's—this being by now the sixties—there was a lot of talk from the pulpit about the evils of extramarital sex and birth control, especially the Pill.

But on Saturday nights, in the parish hall, there was dancing.

In St. Kevin's parish hall, there is a big picture of Blessed Maria Goretti, who died rather than commit a sin of impurity. (One more miracle and she'll be made a saint.)

For the obtuse, four statues of the Virgin Mary.

The girls who'd been at Our Lady of Mercy College dance with the boys who'd been at the Christian Brothers.

Lots of booze. Nothing wrong with booze.

One of the boys takes Marion home. Pokes his wet spaniel tongue into her mouth for a few seconds, then says thank you.

On Saturday afternoons in St. Kevin's parish church, there are weddings. Marion is twice a bridesmaid; she has her hair done in a beehive.

Quickly, quickly, they get married.

The babies begin. So many babies, like loaves and fishes.

The young wives Marion had been at school with would see her sometimes in the street, at church. I gave him his son and now — I tell him — he can jolly well leave me alone. But of course he won't.

Bragging.

No need to leave home, Marion's mother says. She'd be rattling around in the old place on her own. And for what? To get a flat in Bronte, just a short bus ride away? To live in the city? Up at the *Cross*? Ridiculous! Catch a bus *out* to work in the morning? She'd never heard such a bunch of tommyrot in all her days.

Then Magda. Even Magda, who always sneered.

Do you want to be a bridesmaid at a shotgun wedding? Magda asked.

He was from the uni, of course. He's a nice boy, Magda said. I didn't mean this to happen to him.

But Bill was fabulous! He'd gone to Riverview, the poshest school for Catholic boys in Sydney. He was tall, he was handsome, and he was brainy, too. He was going to do graduate work at Columbia University, in America.

Some people, Marion decided, have just about everything. And aren't even grateful.

Magda invited Marion around to tea.

Marion looked into the bedroom. She saw the double bed.

In the lounge room, Riverview Bill was watching TV. In only three months' time they were going overseas.

Columbia should be very interesting, Magda said. She was going to do her Master's, she wasn't going to let the baby slow her down.

She'd write, she promised. She'd tell Marion all about it.

On Friday afternoons, at Gerry Connolly's, they have cakes for afternoon tea. Marion buys them at lunchtime. She really should go on a diet, but you need a few little treats in life, don't you? Around three-thirty she goes into the cubbyhole they call the kitchen and boils the jug. From there, she can see Gerry, staring into space.

What can he be thinking about? John, the late baby, the one who took them by surprise?

This is when The Supremes sing *Oh, how I need your love*, and Gerry Connolly rushes over to Marion, grabs her hand, and puts it right on him. (What would it feel like?) Gerry is wild about her, he can't get any work done he's so crazy for her. He can't stand his wife, the only thing she ever wants to do is say the rosary. And all those kids are getting him down. He's booked a berth on the Southern Aurora, a sleeper, for both of them.

You must come, he cries out, kneeling in front of her. You must, you must.

Late on Friday nights, when her mother has to be asleep, Marion watches TV. She knows all the songs. *I'm a man, yes I am and I can't help but love you so.*

But is her mother really asleep? Marion can feel an ear, growing and growing, coming down the hall.

Even later on Friday nights, Magda's Riverview Bill comes and makes love to her. It was Marion he wanted all along.

Not quite exhausted from the fighting in the streets, Laszlo comes and makes love to her, too. Soon, she will be dead in Parliament Square. (And how Magda will cry out; Magda will be overcome.) In his broken English, Laszlo whispers: sweet little heartbreaker; *foxy lady.*

Laszlo looks a lot like Magda; they are so very much alike.

Marion reads the women's advice columns. Join a church group, they say.

Ha bloody ha, says Marion.

Magda's letters arrive, from America.

Magda and Bill are going to have an open marriage — no more lies, no more pretence.

Magda joins the SDS: I am burning, truly burning, with life, with LIFE, she writes.

I didn't know that people could be so very fine, so careful, so tender and caring about their politics, she writes.

Magda must have a new boyfriend, Marion decides.

It is 1968 and the Tet Offensive; Martin Luther King is assassinated; the buildings at Columbia are occupied and Magda doesn't sleep for a week. Magda abandons the praxis axis and joins the action faction; she has a new lover; she is becoming truly herself, she tells Marion, in the crucible of politics; there is Paris and the events of May; Bobby Kennedy is assassinated; the Prague Spring continues, defiant; Magda has two lovers at once and sleeps not at all.

Dear Marion:

By the time you read this, we'll be in Chicago for the Mobe. As somebody said last week, If you're coming to Chicago, be sure to wear some armor on your hair!!! I don't know what exactly will be going down there but I can tell you there can be no turning back now; our strategy of resistance to this murderous war has been vindicated.

As Teddie says, we have become the *foco,* the small motor that sets the bigger motor of the masses into action.

Last weekend Teddie and Eddie and I managed to get away for the weekend together, just the three of us (four, counting little Laszlo!), to Eddie's parents' place in New Hampshire (they are in Europe for the summer and oblivious, no doubt). Saturday night we did some incredibly mellow dope and watched the stars come out over the mountains. We know we are right on the edge of something big and vast and final—we all three feel it ... who could not feel it these days, in Amerika, and all over the world.

Are you reading about Prague?

Eddie is so good with L.—sings to him, bathes him. Teddie tells him stories—his favourites are about Che and Camilo in the mountains. Teddie says that L. is one far-out child of the revolution. Of two revolutions, I remind him. L. calls them both Deddie, which blows a lot of minds, I can tell you.

How is your mother? You really should (a) move out immediately; (b) pick up a guy and have a far-out, dirty, lost weekend; and (c) get your hands on some dope and blow your mind into a million shining pieces.

Take care,

Love and Peace

Marion watches them being beaten and maced in Chicago. The whole world is watching, they chant.

Typical American exaggeration.

Dear Marion:

I scarcely know how to write this, but it is important. I will try to put it down quietly and soberly for you, dear friend of my heart, so that you can know who I am, and remember.

On Wednesday, last Wednesday, I am in Chicago while the Russian tanks are in Prague. I am in Grant Park with ten thousand others, at a legal rally. The cops charge us, they begin to beat in heads, and the blood begins to flow.

The thing is this: I am running, in Grant Park. I am running towards Michigan Avenue. But I am also running in the streets of Prague. And—and this very, very clearly, with total presence —I am in Budapest. I am home.

I am running with my brother in Rakosi Street, in Ulloi Avenue. I am running with Laszlo in the crowds in front of Parliament Square, I am running with him into the alley behind the Corvin Cinema. I am with him in front of the AVO building on Andrassy Street; I am with him, hiding behind the overturned train cars in Szena Square.

And even more—and this is just as real, just as luminous —Laszlo is here with me. The grey gas is tearing up his lungs. Laszlo is running north with me and we are trying to find a bridge, we have to find a bridge that isn't manned by the Guard with their machine guns.

Marion, I tell you this: he was *right here* and I was *right there.*

Do you understand what I am saying?

While Magda is running in the streets of Chicago, Prague and Budapest, Marion is in Sydney, typing.

She still buys the cakes for afternoon tea on Friday, but on Saturday nights no longer goes to the dance at St. Kevin's parish hall. As her mother says, she is getting too long in the tooth for the boys at St. Kevin's.

Gerry Connolly brings in a new family picture. Caroline, the late, late baby.

Marion and her mother sit in front of the TV and watch what happens at those rock festivals. Marion sees them jumping in the mud. Some of them have very little on.

Disgusting, her mother says.

Who's going to clean all that mess up? That's what I'd like to know, says Marion.

They watch the marches in Australia against the war in Vietnam.

They should crack down on those youngsters who won't go, Marion's mother says. Crack down hard.

Marion, who doesn't agree with the war, not at all, hears herself saying: Dad went, so I don't see why they shouldn't.

4

The rosary group is saving up for a trip. Not to Rome, Lourdes or Fatima. Not even to Knock.

To Southeast Asia.

Marion's mother is going. She's got her orange travel bag from Hopabout Tours.

All the time her mother is away, Marion will have the house to herself. She could do anything.

She could stay out all night and nobody would know.

This is it, Marion tells herself.

If she doesn't get a move on, if somebody doesn't love her, soon, she's going to miss out.

It can happen, does happen. You see them at mass, the women who've missed out. They put on their blue cloaks and go to the Child of Mary meetings—pathetic, dry old virgins.

Some of them must have been quite good-looking once.

How does it happen?

Like this, that's how.

There are other women, the ones Marion watches on TV. They come from the leafy North Shore suburbs, hoity-toity, completely respectable. On Sundays they put on their white gloves and go to church. The Anglican church. Anyway, they run this office for Americans who are in Sydney on leave. You phone them up and tell them what kind you'd like: height, hair colour, everything. The Americans get off the plane from Vietnam, go to the office, and they match you up and they call you.

It's like knitting socks used to be. To keep up morale.

Marion sits at her desk and waits for Gerry Connolly to go out for the *Mirror*. She stares at the phone. (She took the phone number down when it was on the TV.) What if Gerry Connolly came back and she was in the middle of saying brown hair, blue eyes—what *was* she going to say?

Marion's mother gets shingles. They can't get a proper refund at this late date so it is decided: Marion is to go on the Hopabout Tour in her stead.

Gerry Connolly gives her time off work to get her passport.

There is a young man on the tour; he is the only other person about her age. His name is Roy, and he is travelling with his aunt. They are on their way to Hong Kong and Honolulu. This tour is just a tiny side trip, they announce, putting everyone else in their place. The aunt has a loud voice. So does Roy. But he's a man.

They go to see the orchids in Singapore, and Marion thinks he is going to speak to her. Not just like everybody does—isn't it hot and isn't Singapore tiny, fancy having to hang your washing out the window, and no Hills Hoist—but really talk to her.

Roy doesn't come and sit down beside her even though there was a spare seat and you could tell that people were leaving it, almost inviting him. When they leave the bus, he helps the older women. He helps her.

She feels Roy's hand in the small of her back. Cold, disinterested, propelling.

For this, one is supposed to be grateful.

They look at the orchids: shameless, languid, flamboyant, shouting about sex on humid afternoons.

In Malacca, they visit the temples, to see Buddha reclining, Buddha calming the ocean. The rosary group sit together at the back of the bus. Sometimes, as they are travelling along, they finger their beads, which they keep, discreetly, in their pockets.

Roy notices. He gets a singsong going: Jill the dill forgot the Pill and now they have a daughter.

Making mock.

It isn't nice of him and it isn't funny, not really. Thank goodness her mother isn't around.

So much for Roy, the straw man.

Marion is sitting in the dining room of the hotel in Chiang Mai, weighing her chances. There is no other woman in the dining room between the ages of eighteen and thirty. So she must be, by definition, in the running (though even that didn't work with Roy).

He's the first interesting stranger to show up at any of the hotels. He looks younger than she is but sometimes they like you to be a bit older, don't they? He's drinking coffee and he has his eye on her.

She's sure of it. Her stomach's all clenched up, and she wants to go to the toilet but she can't. If she does, he'll think she's leaving. When she gets back, he'll be gone.

Marion forces herself to concentrate on dessert. It's pineapple flummery. You make the jelly with boiling water then let it cool. You put in condensed milk and whisk it all up. It comes out spongy and springy, with little bubbles in it. Here, because it's a posh hotel, they've put some bits of fresh pineapple on top.

He's looking over at her again, she's positive.

Gladly, I will sit here all night, she decides.

I will sit here until hell freezes over, if that's what it takes.

What does it take? Dear God, what does it take?

5

It's early morning and Marion is awake before he is.

She thinks about the low-lying clouds they came through at the end of the flight from KL (she will call it KL, everybody else does). The sun came out, suddenly, on the clouds, and it was so bright, it hurt your eyes to look at them.

She can hear the clatter that's going on down in the kitchens. Doors opening and shutting. Today the tour is scheduled to go into the country, to Lamphun. In Lamphun, she read in the guidebook, there are temples from the eighth and eleventh centuries. After the temples, the tour is going to a factory where they make umbrellas.

Well, she isn't going. She doesn't care about temples and umbrellas. She's going to call down to the desk and say she's still got her tummy upset. For the second day in a row, she's going to stay here, beside him.

Today she'll send Magda a postcard.

Dear Magda, she writes in her head, I have met this soldier who is on R & R from Vietnam.

She can hear Magda saying: It's about time, kiddo.

Dear Magda: He isn't going back to the war.

Magda will understand.

Dear Magda: He has to get away from this murderous war.
He has to get away, to Sweden.

It was a miracle; it was as simple as that. He looked at me
and he believed I was capable of doing such things.

This is how she would describe it, to Magda.

Magda would put back her head and laugh, hah!

The bus group has gone (Roy with them). You can tell they've
gone because it's so quiet in the corridor. Nobody around
except the cleaners. You can hear the cleaners, with their little
trolleys. Going *clunker clunk.*

He didn't know how he was going to do it, get away to
Sweden.

You could tell by the look he got on his face when he talked
about it.

If only he could talk to Magda; Magda would know how
these things were done.

Marion lies in bed thinking in a vague, sleepy way.

He sighs and rolls over in his sleep. She can feel him against
her.

She's listening to the cleaners opening up the rooms and
going in. They leave the doors open when they clean because
they have their trolleys out in the hall.

And at this moment she knows what she can do.

She'll be able to tell Magda. They look a bit alike, him and
Roy. Really, they do.

Him and Roy.

Magda and Laszlo.

She is going to get up, go down the hall, and pinch Roy's
passport. Roy won't have it with him on the bus. He likes to
wear only his little shorts and a singlet. Roy's a showoff.

She's going to swipe that passport and give it to him. She

can give him all her money, too. (Well, most of it.) So he can fly away, fly to Sweden.

Down the hall she goes—it's a breezeway, actually—her caftan billowing.

She's in Roy's room and she's looking about. She's looking in the cupboards, pulling his suitcase out, finding the key to it in the drawer—bloody obvious place—opening the suitcase, sliding her hands around it, and there! in the flap at the top. She's found it.

The passport.

Her hands have lost all feeling; they've gone numb.

As her feet speed along the breezeway, they do not touch the ground at all.

Swiftly, she is running with Magda and Laszlo in Chicago, she is running with them in Prague, in the streets of Budapest. In front of the AVO building, into the alley behind the Corvin Cinema.

She is with Laszlo in the bloodbath at Parliament Square.

She is with Magda, twelve hours in the swamp.

A bit player in the crowd scene of history. In the show, at last.

Two: Rowing to Sweden

1

He's on the train and he's thinking about the guy who gives Yossarian the money. Go now for God's sake and hurry, this dude says to Yossarian.

It had happened to him, just like that. She'd given him some money. And she'd gotten him that passport. That passport was about to come in mighty handy.

It must be nice in Sweden now, this other guy says to Yossarian. The girls are sweet and the people are so advanced.

Jungle green green green. It was going by, he was on his way. Green green, I'm going away to where the grass is greener still. It was going to be fucking cold in Sweden, he didn't like the cold. But the girls would be sweet.

He has to get out to the airport in Bangkok and use that Aussie passport. Do you have enough baht for the taxicab? she wanted to know.

Did they have an airline that went straight to Sweden? She thought that maybe they had one that went to Paris.

He'd stay away from Braniff. He'd come to Nam on Braniff. Braniff always pulls out on time, joke. There were these stewardesses handing out Cokes and little bags of nuts and they were taking him to the war.

If he couldn't get a plane that went straight to Sweden he'd get one that went to Paris. What if they didn't go to Paris? What if they just went to Germany or someplace like that? He wished he knew the names of some towns in Germany. He didn't know squat about Germany. He knew the names of some of the bases but that was the last thing he was going to need, some gigunda sonofabitch army base.

He was going to keep his cool. He was going to keep his cool, all the way through.

Travis, Guam, Bien Hoa. Now Bangkok, Paris maybe, Stockholm.

It was freaking weird, man. Before all this he'd been to Seattle twice. He'd seen the Space Needle.

He'd already finished eating when they came in. He got his coffee and he watched them.

A bus tour, shit yes. Speaking English, but not English. What would they be? Australians? Maybe. Arty'd had an Australian chick when he was on R & R in Hong Kong. Just like back home, he said, shy and pink at first then all red and juicy later.

He stirred his coffee and checked them out. Old dudes with their wives. Women on their own, old. Two young kids with their parents. One young guy, maybe a few years older than he was.

Then her.

She sat down beside two of the old dames on their own. She didn't sit down at the other table, where the young guy was, nothing doing between them. You could tell by the way she looked at him. He was ordering for his whole table. Loud, she thinks he's loud. Scared by noises most likely.

Arty'd had a picture of this Australian chick. One of those pictures you take in the little booth in the bus station. Arty kept it in a plastic thing in his pocket. The big pocket. The big pocket on the right-hand side of his jungle utilities.

This chick'd sent Arty a Peace sign. Arty had it in his boonie hat.

Arty was short, real short.

Arty and Mike used to shoot the shit a lot. They both came from Idaho, that was why.

Arty told Mike he'd made this chick in the elevator by the time they'd got to the eleventh floor. Got her all lined up, anyways, in eleven floors flat. Was that just bullshit or was it for real?

Just look at her over there, being so polite.

Arty'd hit on a booby trap.

Look at her, using her knife as well as her fork.

On some nasty red hill. Blew his ass to kingdom come.

He'd blown the first two nights already. Two whole nights of not getting laid, lying on his bed looking at the ceiling, not thinking about Mike and Mitzie, not thinking about them.

He hadn't wanted Bangkok, he'd wanted Hawaii. But after what had gone down he'd just got on the first thing out. Friends in low places.

Bangkok was a downer, bar girls all over in Bangkok, but he didn't want bar girls, there were times he couldn't get into bar girls.

And there she was. Eating dessert now. He'd had a shower and everything, before he left the guesthouse, just as well.

He'd gone to the train station in Bangkok and he didn't know what the fuck he was doing, he hadn't thought it through, he just caught the next train out and ended up in this place.

Chiang Mai.

Those pamphlet things said the place was full of temples. Wat this and Wat that. Wat Suan Dok. At first he thought it said Wat Susan Dork. He didn't want Wats, nossir. Put a *T* in front of that and you had what he wanted. And what he wanted you simply could not get. There were nurses, of course, but they wouldn't give you the time of day. If you were some asshole lifer down at Long Binh, then maybe.

Like Mike said, there was only one memorable thing you could get in the Republic of Vietnam besides wasted. Heavy shit and plenty of it any old time you wanted.

Mike'd sit on the sandbags and Mitzie'd sit in his shade, going after her fleas. Mike'd read bits of *Catch 22*. Mike knew whole chunks of *Catch 22* off by heart. Specially the last bits, where Yossarian is rowing to Sweden, and, goddamn it, making it.

I've got responsibilities now, Yossarian says, I've got to get to Sweden. It's a geographic impossibility to get there from here, this other dude says. And Yossarian says: at least I'll be trying.

When he went on R & R, Mike said, that'd be it. Good-bye, KIA Travel.

Mike said he'd go to Hawaii, party some, then fly on to Seattle. Once you got to Seattle, Mike said, all you had to do was follow your nose. As soon as he'd got fixed up, Mike was going to let him know what to do and he'd be gone too. With the Mitz. They weren't going to leave the Mitz behind, no way.

But here he was, instead. And he was travelling light. No Mike and no Mitzie. As soon as he'd gotten himself laid he was rowing to Sweden. At least he'd be trying.

2

After he'd heard about Mike and Mitzie, he'd gone back to the hooch to lie down. He felt so freaking tired. It went through his mind that now he'd paid, he could hold his head up, he'd paid. But it didn't work like that, he knew better than that.

Back at the hooch some fucking new guy was playing "Bridge over Troubled Waters." He wished to Christ he wasn't playing that thing.

Still and all he expected to see them, Mike and Mitzie. He looked up and he expected to see them come into the hooch. He really expected that.

When he first met Mike, he told him you had to stop them someplace.

Mike just went uh huh, uh huh, uh huh.

He'd told Arty, too: You had to stop them someplace.

Arty punched him, and laughed. It was Arty's first day back at battalion after weeks in the bush. Arty was goofing off.

Arty was rolling on the ground with him. They were grabbing each other, sort of wrestling, and laughing. Saigon tomorrow, Spokane next, Arty was shouting. The Mitz was charging about, joining in. Mike started to sing one of his songs: So long Mommie, I'm off to get a commie. Then Art was just sitting on top of him and they were all laughing/barking, feeling pretty good.

He was looking at Arty's jungle boots. They'd gone that sickly orange colour.

Why was it Arty out there in the boonies and not him?

Loudmouth at the other table had fucked off. The old dames were leaving the chick's table. She was ordering some more coffee. Good. Excellent, in fact.

She was sitting at the table on her own.

He was going to be in luck for once, he could feel it. It was a long time since Susan. Back in Spokane, he and Susan had been going together since grade ten, he could hardly remember how it was when he first made it with her.

He hoped he wasn't going to blow this.

Go over there and say you'd like to buy her a drink, ask her her name and that.

Mike used to say: You tell them you want to kiss their breasts. Turns them to batter, saying that.

But what do you say first? I mean, you just don't lean over and say, I'd like to kiss your breasts. Not straight off.

She looked at me!

I swear, clear as day, she looked right over here.

Yes, man, she looked at me.

Tell them they're beautiful, they love to hear they're beautiful. Christ, they *are* beautiful.

She was looking over at him again. She was.

Nice little breasts, she'd have those sweet soft warm little breasts with faint blue veins. It made him weak to think of them.

Last time he'd been home with Susan, she'd wanted him to go here, go there, see family all the time. He told Susan he didn't give a rat's ass about going on some dipshit picnic with her whole family. I mean, her parents were coming.

And she starts this thing, I feel I don't know you any more, I just don't know you any more. Jesus H. Christ.

It was crazy, of course, and no way he'd say this to anyone, but he knew by now he was carrying them inside him, Mike and Mitzie. He had them inside him, and he was carrying them around with him. He'd hear Mike talk to him, he'd hear Mike's voice that clearly. And he'd see the Mitz looking up at him with those eyes of hers that said, *I'm glad, I'm glad, I'm glad.*

Go over to her, man. Smile, act real nice now. Don't talk too loud and don't swear. Just ask if you can sit down, say may I. Sit down and be sure to ask her about herself. Where has she been? Did she like all those Wats? Sure she would, she'd like them.

Tell her about being on base. Say you checked the supplies and things. You made sure they got out to the LZs. Call them landing zones so she'll know what you're talking about.

Don't mention your best buddy Mike, over at GR point. She won't want to know about Graves Registration, man. And can the KIAs. She won't want to be hearing about no KIAs. Tell her you're on R & R and the Wats are very beautiful although you haven't seen them yet. But the most beautiful thing you've seen since you left Travis is her. The most beautiful. She'll like that.

And get a move on, man, get your ass in gear. She's been sitting there and sitting there and waiting for you to get off your butt. Go to it, man.

It wasn't all that hard, really. She looked up and she blushed. Christ, how long since he'd seen a chick blush real nice like that. And for *him*. And she said, yes, she'd like a drink from the bar. Marion, her name was Marion, he made a mental note. They went to the bar and he said, Marion, what would you like? And she said, white wine.

White wine. He'd forgotten all about white wine. It sat there in its little glass and the glass went all nice and frosty.

He had a beer himself.

And she asked, Are you a student travelling round?

Travelling round. He couldn't get over it, it was heavy duty, man, it was so long since he'd had to deal with this kind of thing.

He told her he was on R & R and she knew what he meant.

Oh, she said, I'm sorry. You must think I'm silly.

Oh no, he said. No. And shook his head, and smiled at her.

She smiled back at him. At first I thought you were Roy, she said. You look a lot like him.

Roy's this guy on the tour. Roy, it turns out, is Loudmouth at the other table.

She liked him, he could tell. They put out these vibes, man, Arty'd said, and you don't have to say a thing. You could feel them hanging in the air. You could reach out and take a hold of them. The vibes.

But sooner or later, Arty'd said, they just have to know. They start squirming in their seats, working themselves up to ask. They don't ask right out, but you can see them thinking it.

Have you wasted anyone?

This Marion, she squirmed around a bit and she asked him: Were you in the fighting?

Meaning.

I'm on base, he said.

He saw her shoulders relax a little. I mean, she wouldn't want to go climbing into bed with some horny young killer, now would she?

Mike'd say: What if the President, the Congress and the generals and the colonels and all of them believe, really believe, mind you, that they're doing right. And what if it's just the asshole at the end of the line who can see they're full of it?

About like that.

Mike knew how to say things, he was older. Mike'd done two years at junior college.

Mike said you couldn't expect the army to know its ass from a hole in the ground, it was the army. But what about all those fancy folks back home with their degrees and shit? In foreign relations and everything. Experts, they were. What about them?

He had to concentrate on the job in hand. At the moment she was just sitting there drinking her white wine, with her legs together under the bar.

They couldn't sit here drinking all night. See her up to her room? He couldn't ask if he could come in for coffee. Use the washroom? Maybe. He'd kiss her at the door. That might lead to something or it might not.

Sure she liked him. That didn't mean she'd haul him into her room and rip all her clothes off pronto. What if she'd only go for a nighty-night kiss and catch you tomorrow? He didn't have the time.

Tonight, he had to make his move tonight. Round about now.

She worked in an office in this place called Sydney.

He thought he'd heard of Sydney. Come to think of it he was nearly sure he'd heard of it.

It's a big city, she said. The biggest in the country.

Bigger than Spokane, I guess, he said.

They both laughed.

She wanted to laugh, that was good. And she got a deliberate look on her face and said yes, she'd like another glass of white wine, thank you very much.

The more white wine the better. You better believe it.

Then she brought her face up to his and — can you beat this — she asked: Have you lost anyone close to you?

The dark, all around him. The dark it got out there when there was no moon. You couldn't see your hand in front of your face. Charlie was out there. Charlie knew his way around in the dark.

He lived there.

3

He reached over and he put his hand on her leg. She got a bit red in the face. Then, carefully, she put her hand on his. As soon as he felt her do that, he knew — she'd decided, yes. And he nearly jumped, even though he'd been hoping for it. Migod it was going to be easy, he never expected it would be that easy. All he had to do was reach down and turn her hand over and rub his thumb up and down that fleshy part.

Wet, ah yes, very wet. But tight. Tight as a mouse hole.

He figured it out. Christ! He'd never had anyone's cherry before. Susan had done it with Frankie Mankiewicz, with Susan it'd been the first time for him but not for her.

He was embarrassed. How old was she anyway? Old. Must be twenty-three or -four at least.

He'd never done this before. Was he going to be able to do it right? Give her a fine time, a real fine time.

Gently, taking care, he rubbed his hands across her breasts. He said it: I want to kiss your breasts. And she liked that, she made a little noise.

Then slowly — no hurrying this, he was just going to have to wait, for his — he moved down her belly, down and down, to get a taste of her. She panicked a bit and pushed on his head with her hands. So he was quiet for a while. Just stroked her thighs. Told her she was beautiful. And she calmed right down. She got into it, and yes, oh yes. When he slipped in she was out of her mind, or just about.

It wasn't difficult at all. Or not very.

He lay down beside her and she snuggled up under his arm, knowing how. You're a natural, kid, he said, pleased with himself, pleased with her. They'd done okay. They'd done quite nicely, if he did say so himself.

He could smell her hair. Her clean-smelling shampoo.

He felt so tired, so very tired, lying quietly there beside her, like that.

He showed her the photographs, Mike and Mitzie. In the first one, they were in front of Graves, but you couldn't tell that from the photo. Mike was holding Mitzie in his arms. Then there was Mitzie, playing frisbee with the guys. Mitzie at the entrance to the hooch. "Pooch and hooch," Mike had written on the back of that one.

There were two hooches, he explained to her. The bunker was in between. You have to go into one of the hooches to get to the bunker.

Mitzie had her steak.

She had her shots.

She had her frisbee.

Mitzie had her belly tickled.

Mike got her wormed.

She knew all the best places to catch the shade.

All the guys loved Mitzie.

But Mike worried about her, a lot. What if, uh, what if she was left running around with her little guts all hanging out?

Mike worried about that. Then this guy comes back from Long Binh one day with some jab Mike could give Mitzie if she needed it. If she needed to be, you know, put to sleep.

Mike'd found her in the dump outside the perimeter, just an itty-bitty little thing, sniffing around the slops. He'd put

her in the flatbed and got her over to GR point and then he
went and got her something to eat. She was Mike's pooch,
really. She leapt that high for him. She went everywhere with
him, she sat up in that truck and she looked out, real happy.

Mitz was over at GR point with Mike most of the time.
The Mitz liked to lie by the reefers.

Reefers?

Reefers are these Conex container things. They have a gen-
erator to keep the bodies cool.

She looked scared.

He shouldn't have explained to her about the GR point, or
the reefers.

He shut up fast.

What happened? she wanted to know.

He shrugged and turned away. She moved her hand around
to the back of his neck, rubbed him there.

Let's get up and go out, she said. Maybe we should go to
the cultural centre, she said, looking in her guidebooks. Or to
the university. The roofs of the university are paved with gold,
she said. It says here.

They went out walking. For some crazy reason the guesthouse he'd booked into gave you a bike, for free. So he walked
alongside her, pushing this bike, and it was like he was back
in high school again, walking Susan home.

They found a park by the river. The Ping River, she said.
But this other guidebook called it the Meping. Like the
Mekong, she goes on. Maybe Me means river, what do you
think?

He didn't know. Sometimes he didn't know what to say to
her.

Do you have a river in Sydney? he asked. Trying.

She laughed.

He must've said something dumb.

We have a harbour, she said. A big one.

Oh, he said. We have a river in Spokane. The Spokane
River.

And she said: The harbour is called the Sydney Harbour.

Very original all round, he said.

At that, they could both laugh.

He moved over on the bench, to be closer to her. He put his arms around her. Both arms.

She's more interested in this than in small talk, he thought, relieved. Well, he had plenty of this. He could give her plenty of this.

Let's go back to the hotel, he said.

He told her he was getting out, not going back. At the end of his R & R he was going to Sweden.

How are you going to get there? she asked.

How was he going to get there?

Go to Tokyo, maybe. Mike'd told him about these sailors who met in a coffeehouse in Tokyo and decided to desert. Mike said some underground group in Japan helped them. They'd got them to Russia, and then finally to Sweden.

How are you going to find this underground group? she asked.

He didn't know. He couldn't remember the name of the group, it was some real weird name. He'd have to find that coffeehouse first.

He wasn't sure what a coffeehouse in Japan looked like. Was it like the ones near the bases back home? Or did it have Joan Baez playing and college kids sitting around drinking those fancy coffees with the froth on top? In Japan?

He should've paid more attention to Mike. Anyways, he should've gone to Hawaii. From Hawaii you could step on a plane to Seattle and in Seattle he'd know what to do. He was *born* in Washington, for shit's sake.

He lay on the bed, worrying.

How do you feel, they ask Yossarian, just before he splits. Fine, Yossarian says. Then he says, no, I'm frightened. That's good, this other guy says, it shows you're still alive.

Well, he was still alive, and he was frightened.

Arty and Mike and Mitzie had bought the farm and he was still alive.

Figure that one out.

4

He'd been in-country eight weeks and he'd pulled guard duty on the perimeter.

Guard duty is fucking boring, man, everyone knows that. You're out there and you're bored shitless. You beat off and you're bored shitless again.

He must've dozed off because next thing he knew the perimeter kind of exploded. Christ, the noise! He had this M-60, and he didn't know where the fuck or what the fuck but something exploded and then he was firing it, man, he was firing it and firing it.

Next morning there's some guts going loop-de-loop in the wire. The other one's lying very neat, like he's curled up asleep. Only his head's missing.

Back in the hooch he lay and stared at the ceiling. If you could call it a ceiling. Mitzie came in, nosing about.

Mike said: Get on up there with him, Mitzie. Go on, girl, get up there.

And she did. She got up beside him and settled down, cosy. Pretty soon his hand came out and he was rubbing Mitzie's belly, her tiny pooch nipples.

Mike said: Look at Mitzie, she's got that real spaced-out look on her face.

What they'd have done without the Mitz, he didn't know.

You'll feel guilty, this guy says to Yossarian. Your conscience will give you a bad time. Good for my conscience, says Yossarian. I wouldn't want to live without misgivings.

Guilty about *getting out*?

Mike said "misgivings" was one candy-ass word.

They're at chow one day and these guys at the next table are talking:

His nuts, man. The dink's nuts.

Little fuckers.

You can crank up a lot of voltage on a jeep battery.

The little fucker's little fuckers.

Put your foot on the gas and hey presto.

A twelve-volt jeep battery.

Guaranfuckinteed.

Like a charm, my man.

Eat your heart out, Ma Bell.

They say this like they're ordering root beer or something.

She came out of the shower and she was all steamed up and she looked so pink and naked he couldn't believe it. She was standing right there with nothing on, smiling for him, and it was too much, he felt like crying, he really did.

Come over here, he said.

He was showing her things. Like how to touch him.

It helped, oh yes, it helped.

He wakes up and she's looking at him.

I didn't want to wake you, she says.

Didn't want to wake him. Maybe he'd turn into some crazy and throttle her. That's what they all thought now, Arty said. They were afraid.

She's full of something, she's bursting with it, you can tell.

Her eyes are big like she's been doing some speed. Arty said hookers in Europe used to do some drug or other to make their eyes go all big. Mike said, wasn't any different nowdays, half the time a pro was out of her mind on some shit or other. How come they knew all about hookers and he didn't? It never really occurred to him to go with a pro back home. He wasn't too swift, he knew it.

I got you his passport, she says.

The man on the tour, she says, the one who looks like you. You remember. Loudmouth. He looks enough like you. Really, he does. The photo would have been taken a few years ago, anyway.

Take the passport, she says.

I'll give you some money, she says. I've got some money.

You have the money, she says. Take the passport and go. They won't notice it's missing until after you're gone.

It was crazy crazy crazy but he knew in a flash that Mike had arranged all this. For her to be there, for her to get him the passport.

She looked lovely, with those big hooker eyes.

She gleamed.

You're a sweet little angel, he said, and I love the way you spread your wings.

They went back to the guesthouse off Huai Kaeo Road. They had to keep looking at the map to find it, because the street signs were in Thai.

He packed up and he left the bike, and they went to the train station.

He was grateful. He truly was. He told her so.

But she didn't want grateful.

Already she had begun to look at him with eyes that hoped for things.

Like Arty said: You meet a chick and ball her, both of you having a real fine time, and next morning you wake up and she's writing her first name with your last, holding it out in front of her to see how it looks. Next thing you know she's thinking about furniture. Furniture, man. Tables, chairs, chesterfields, bedroom fixings. *Garden* furniture.

But he was going, he was getting out. He felt easier somehow, knowing he was leaving her. In a few hours he'd be gone.

They sat on a bench and he talked about the war.

5

It was an ordinary day in the Republic of Vietnam. He was getting some stuff together for the choppers. Mike and Mitzie were down at GR point, as usual. He had his transistor going.

"By the Time I Get to Phoenix," followed by "Bridge over Troubled Waters."

By the time I get to Hawaii, he was thinking, I will lay me down.

He could see the big clouds piling on top of the hills behind the airstrip. It was one of the worst things, he'd decided, the way this place could be beautiful.

As a kid back in Spokane he'd had this thing about the jungle. He'd seen it at the movies.

He's going up this river in the middle of the jungle someplace, in a slow old boat. You can hear the chug chug chug of the motor. You can hear birds going skwark skwark. He's just lying there, floating up the river. There's this haze all around. And the smell of jungle flowers. Flowers from the jungle, heavy and sweet.

The Nam ruined all that. Jungle: the smell of shit, burning.

He'd been excited at first. When they landed at Bien Hoa and he felt the jungle, felt it splash over him like a can of wet paint, he'd thought: Wow, this is it, I'm in the jungle now. And it turned him on, it really did, even though he was going to the war.

It was so different from Spokane. It can get mighty cold in Spokane. It gets so crispy cold you can bite it.

This day, he's loading up Willie Peter mortars, white phosphorus, that is. He's moving Willie P from point A to point B. He knows what WP does, he isn't completely stupid. WP burns and burns and won't stop burning until it's burned right through. So long as it has contact with air, WP burns.

He's thinking about all this, he's loading up the stuff, he's looking up at the great big clouds piling up on the hills. Mother-puffers, he calls them. Big mother-puffers.

In his head he's going blabber blabber blab as usual.

They tell you in school how many yards of guts you've got inside, all tucked up. When you see that shit hanging out like ropy Jello-O, it's weird, you can't help but think, so that's what it's like inside.

The folks back home were all in favour of sending him over here so's he could figure out things like that. Well thanks, folks. Thanks a whole bunch.

Blabber blabber blab.

Round about this time, a chopper crashes into a nearby hill. They medevac some guys out but for some reason known only to the army—meaning, for no reason at all—they leave the KIAs behind. And Mike's NCO over at Graves decides they have to go get them in.

So Mike and Mitzie drive off in the mortuary GR flatbed to go get in the KIAs. Eddie Diaz was supposed to go too but he was taking a crap.

Mike would've loaded the KIAs up on his own. Mitz would have been out of the truck, running around, checking things out. When Mike got back in the truck he would've opened the passenger door and called: C'mon Mitzie, time to move it.

The Mitz, she'd have come right away. She would've gone anywhere with Mike, and besides, she was crazy about that truck.

Sometimes, when Mike thought no one was watching, he'd bend down and kiss Miss Mitzie's bony head.

Did he do that? Maybe he just petted her some when he leaned over to close the door.

Driving back to base they hit a mine, one motherfucker, almost 175 pounds. Not meant for some shitty little load of KIAs, meant for the armored cavalry, for sure.

This thing leaves a hole in the ground about eight feet deep and the size of your mom and dad's bedroom back home.

The KIAs are blown to shit one more time.

Eddie Diaz has to go out and get them in.

They probably won't know it's missing until they're leaving Bangkok, she says, for about the twentieth time. He's on the train platform now, he's just about to get on the train.

One more day left here, then three whole days in Bangkok. You'll be in Stockholm by then, she says. Or Paris at the least, she says.

Over and over, she looks in the passport.

Royden Dangar, the name. Some weird name.

Born, 1945. Older than him.

Chatswood, New South Wales.

It's a suburb of Sydney, she says.

Not that they'll ask, she goes on. They never ask, they just look. Say yes and no. Say them quietly so they won't notice that accent. You're on a holiday. Say "holiday" quickly, don't drag it out. Maybe you can whisper. Say you've got a sore throat; nobody has an accent when they whisper. Once you're on the plane, no worries. Call them mate. That's a good idea. Say, yes mate, no mate.

She says all these things like she's trying to be some experienced gangster. Though you can tell she's just thinking them up this minute.

All flushed and excited, like she's trying to come.

Oh baby, he says. I love you, baby.

Christ, how she goes for that. How she smiles and sobs at the same time. How she waves and waves.

Any dude in Vietnam or with orders for the war zone could be a political refugee in Sweden, Mike said.

He didn't much like the sound of that word, refugee. He hoped he'd get enough to eat. What do they eat in Sweden, anyway?

He hoped he wasn't going to fuck this up.

He had to be on his toes, every minute.

But he was going to be okay, he just knew it. Now that he and Mike and the Mitz were in this rowboat. They'd made it to the boat and now all they had to do was row easy, row easy and watch the jungle going by.

There were two other dudes in the boat. One of them didn't have a head but he was neat and quiet, no problem. The other one had his guts trailing out behind the boat, trailing in the river.

They were going to make it, he knew it. It was so peaceful, rowing to Sweden. He was going downstream with this haze all around.

Those other two just sat there. He and Mike were the ones doing the rowing.

To Be There
with You

WATER, the smell of brown water, its presence all around. On the one side, the river, meeting the ocean, taking its time. On the other, the South China Sea, with its small surf.

I sit in the hotel room and I wait for Ron.

When I went to that country I took with me one newspaper clipping. It was a photo of a Buddhist monk, who in the protests of the year before had poured gasoline over himself and burned to death.

I pinned it on the wall of the hotel room, as a challenge. Quickly, it was discoloured by the humidity; it curled at the edges.

The city had by this time become a series of clichés. It was these clichés I sent home, once more. You remember: the pedicabs, the ox carts, the cyclos, the capricious streams of laneless traffic, the taxi fleet of neurotic blue-and-cream Renaults, the pall of exhaust. The big gutters at the sides of the streets, pungent. The water sellers with their panniers balanced on bamboo sticks across their shoulders; the shoeshine boys; the prostitutes in miniskirts. The bars and massage parlours along Tu Do; the clapped-out tamarinds. The checkpoints, the flaking plaster on the buildings at the heart of town, the hotels— Graham Greene's old Continental and the thin, new Caravelle, where the Australian embassy was located.

I described these things and I looked at the Buddhist monk. And I felt discouraged.

Two things I did not write about:

The people who lived there. What did they talk about when they talked with one another?

The corruption of unknowing. (*Did the people of Vietnam use lanterns of stone?*)

It was a relief to go down to Vung Tau, where the Australian forces were headquartered.

The room I finally found in Vung Tau was everything it should have been. It had vile plumbing and dubious bedding. Everywhere, plants in pots. And tiny wrought-iron balconies that looked out towards the water (you couldn't see it, but you knew it was there). After Saigon, Vung Tau was wonderful.

It was a bit embarrassing, in this French colonial setting, to be happy with Ron. Ron was in the regular army. I should not have approved. It was the men who'd been drafted I felt for— the nashos, the national servicemen, conscripts in a foreign war they knew nothing about.

In my letters home to friends I changed Ron into a French journalist. I had met him, I claimed, in the Saigon offices of *La Presse*. The only trouble with Henri, I wrote, is that he talks all the time.

One of the best thing about being in Vungers was that I didn't have to go to the daily briefings. In Saigon, I was terrified— not of the war, but of the press corps.

There were hundreds of accredited correspondents in Saigon; they came from all around the world. There were women among them, some of whom were really famous. They were the ones who scared me the most. With the men, I could excuse myself.

But the women. I trembled.

Every day from about two o'clock onwards, a sinking feeling set in. Around three o'clock I'd decide to skip. From then until shortly before four I'd feel as if a mighty load had been lifted from me. From four onwards, I imagined myself taking part, and wished I were there.

I should be walking along Nguyen Hue to reach the room above the art gallery. I should be going up the steep stairs, choosing one of the hard, fold-up chairs, preferably near the fan. I should be examining the roneoed sheet that gave the daily statistics.

This was the Vietnamese briefing, and it was usually over within a few minutes. Nobody was interested in what the Vietnamese had to say about the war.

The twenty minutes between four-forty and five o'clock were the worst. This was when the journalists chatted with one another as they dawdled over to the main event—the briefing at JUSPAO, the Joint U.S. Public Affairs Office, just down the street.

The Free World briefing.

At JUSPAO there was the relief of air conditioning, there was ice water, there were comfortable chairs.

I saw myself, with Henri, moving easily among the journalists handing their passes to the marine at the door. The two of us, part of the crowd, making our way through the JUSPAO corridors to the auditorium at the back of the building. At the entrance to the auditorium we pick up the daily handouts, and I look to see if there are any Australian ones. I have some quick, perceptive thing to say. Henri laughs. After the briefing we are part of the crowd again, going off to the top floor next door, to eat frozen food flown in from the States. And to complain about it, later.

I should have been there for the show itself, which I did enjoy. First, the chief of the U.S. mission usually came on and made a few remarks. Against the curtained stage, he looked exactly like the master of ceremonies. Then the colonels gave a spiel, ground briefing, air briefing, complete with slides and coloured maps, no expenses spared. They spoke in a dense military argot that I did not understand.

Then came the best bit: the questions. (I never asked a question myself.) Question time often generated a fair bit of snarling, usually from the U.S. journalists.

Once or twice, during question time, the entire auditorium would be seized with something alert, strained. I didn't know what it was, but it felt like the hairs going up on a dog's back.

Atrocities were not yet defined as news. News, at that time, was numbers: 189 Reds die in three battles.

I wrote in my diary: I look at Ron and my bones turn to milk.

Then: No, no, that sounds like dog food.

And later: D.H. was right but T.E. probably more Ron's man.

I kiss him and my mouth shivers.

Start with what you've got, they'd told me back home. Always get the names of the boys' hometowns. Find out how many sisters and brothers they have, what the father does. See if any of the country papers are buying.

The Singapore-based correspondent who was my main contact described my presence in Vietnam as a "colossal brass-up." He found out about Ron, and said, "Now we'll get some in-depth coverage, nudge nudge."

Each time Ron was coming down from the Dat I was busy all day (clean the room, buy French pastries and bottles of Coke, paint nails — hands and feet, iron clothes, etc.). Ron let me know he simply couldn't get over his good luck: here he'd found someone to be with who wasn't a prostitute. He didn't have to worry about getting the jack.

I washed my hair and imagined Ron, thirty kilometres away, having his shower. Getting clean for me, safely back from the bush. Again.

I was the only woman he'd ever slept with besides Shirl. So he said, and I believed him. He was shocked by the prostitutes; a lot of the soldiers were, especially the ones who used them. (They were a pretty straightlaced bunch, the Aussie soldiers.)

There were women and children fighting them. They couldn't get over it.

While I wait for Ron, I look at myself in the mirror.

I love you, I say to the mirror, to Ron, who is not yet here.

Is this how love feels?

Vung Tau juts out into the sea like a small boot.

In the crowded front beach area there is a persistent feeling of holiday. Lots of Aussies, steady boozers all, and Yanks on their in-country R & R. There are Koreans, and there are the South Vietnamese themselves. And moving among them, invisible, are the VC. For nobody denies that the VC, too, routinely use Vung Tau for R & R.

On the front beach evenings begin early, with a kind of nervy gaiety. By night's end that has deteriorated into something thick and heavy and tangled. You can smell the beer soaking into the dirt. You are forced to listen to the song declaring, with a hideous, accurate sentimentality, that the carnival is over.

On the back beaches the soldiers settled in, and were kept busy protecting their equipment from the sand.

Vung Tau was easy to write about: details piled up without effort. I visited the orphanage the soldiers were restoring in a nearby village; I interviewed the surgical team at Le Loi Hospital; I wrote about Villa 44, the rest and convalescence centre; I mentioned the Grand, the main watering hole. The town, I claimed, had "a crumbling French ambience." The young Vietnamese women in their *ao dais* "seemed to float along the boulevard." That gave me particular pleasure, using the word, boulevard. Me, a kid from Australia.

I produced these lying, partial stories and at first I was happy enough to do so. I believed I was getting somewhere. I wrote the way the soldiers wrote letters home. Only they knew what they were censoring, and I did not.

Once that fact became clear to me, I became preoccupied with it.

Back home, it was a Liberal prime minister who said, "You are right to be where you are and we are right to be there with you." They wanted to suck up to the Yanks.

But I liked the soldiers. They were nice and ordinary and scared. I knew what their homes were like on Saturday afternoon: a radio would be blaring the races. If they were Sydney boys, I knew what football teams they cheered for, what beaches they went to.

How they'd eat fruitcake and drink beer on a hot December afternoon.

What Mum would cook for tea and where she'd hang her apron, how Mum had made that apron herself and trimmed it with a bit of rickrack.

What sort of tin Nanna kept her biscuits in. What kind of biscuits they'd be, how they'd taste.

It was just as well I knew something about the soldiers, I reassured myself. Because they told me nothing. Nothing at all.

I am up at the lines at Nui Dat. I am talking to men just back from the bush. I stand in front of them in my miniskirt, with my long young legs. I ask them to tell me all about the war.

Before Ron, I'd had one other lover, and considered myself experienced. With him, love had been an overwhelming project, constructed out of words. I would rehearse the words, analyse and revise them, finding them ill-suited to the huge task.

With Ron there was silence. His body understood. We could sit in two separate chairs and feel whatever it was, humming back and forth.

Because the soldiers told me nothing, I had to make do with geography.

Leaving Nui Dat, one sees the red soils of the dry rolling hills with their rubber, banana and coffee plantations give way to a brief flowering of tender green paddies which are, as we approach Vung Tau, suddenly usurped by the salt marshes and mangroves in their drab army colours.

I tried again.

Nui Dat, which means "small hills," is actually located in a rubber plantation, I chirruped. Above the camp one sees the Nui Thi Vai, the mountains that the soldiers have dubbed the Warbies, after the Warburtons, in the state of Victoria.

I even managed quotes: "Conditions are fair enough, really. You don't expect the Ritz."

We had been lovers in a past life, I decided. In some smoky Celtic cottage, in a valley full of mild rain, I had waited quietly for him.

Even in that life, he'd been married.

There wasn't any question of my mucking things up with Shirl.

I am sitting with Ron in the courtyard of the hotel at Vung Tau. We are reading the *Sydney Morning Herald*.

Ron is reading about what some of the Labor politicians are saying about the war. He looks cranky. Ron's been a Labor man all his life.

I am reading the review section. It is quoting famous writers on the U.S. involvement in Vietnam. (There's a new book out.) I like the Pinter quote: "They were wrong to go in, but they did. Now they should get out, but they won't."

Might come in handy some day, I think. I copy it into my diary.

"What's that you're writing?" Ron asks.

"Nothing," I say. "Nothing."

What does he do out there in the war? I picture him: he is in a VC village. He takes a grenade from his body, pulls the pin out, and chucks it down the well. (Is that what they do? They do use a hand grenade for something like this, don't they?)

I can see him walking away, through the village, away from the ruined well. He has now grown very tall; he walks in giant boots.

These images come to me when I am moving my hands over his body.

I wonder if Shirl reads my pieces. Shirl is sitting in her kitchen, in the Sydney suburb of Bexley North. Her kitchen smells of white toast and Vegemite and kids. The neighbours are proud of Shirl, coping on her own with the two kiddies. Shirl is proud of Ron, her soldier, her man.

It is, after all, no more than a year since the Battle of Long Tan. And at Long Tan we won by 245 to 18. We Australians excel at outdoor activities of all kinds.

I dream of writing something like that, especially for Shirl.

Everyone had a camera; cameras were all the rage. There was this photo of Ron and me and his best mate, Johnno. We are in the courtyard of the hotel at Vungers. Ron has his arms around my shoulders. Johnno is beside him, holding up a beer, putting on the big bronzed Anzac act. Ron is looking at me, sort of smiling.

I swear, if you had seen that photo, you would have said he loved me.

At first it seemed that there was Ron with me and the war on one side, and Shirl and the kids back home on the other. As the weeks went by it felt different. On the one hand there was Shirl at home and me in Vungers. On the other hand, there was the war. At this rate, I told myself, I'd never be *bao chi*, a proper journalist.

Beer left Ron as tightlipped as ever, so I got my hands on some marijuana. Ron agreed to give it a go.

It made him completely paralytic. He sat rooted to his chair, unable to move. From time to time he said, "Ratshit, mate. Ratshit."

It was a profound truth. But I was no further ahead.

Sometimes after sex he did get a tiny bit talkative. Like this:

"We were going down this bloody hill and we walked straight into the noggies. Right on top of them."

"And, and?" I urged.

"Felt a bit sorry for them really. Poor bastards. Having their smoko."

"I love you," I say to Ron.

Ron was older than the man I'd been with before and his big heavy body pressed down upon me without apology.

(Do I love him, do I, really?)

Having been brought up Catholic I believe in the power words can have, particularly when repeated.

"I love you, Ron."

He gives a short, tight laugh.

Being there, I am forced to consider the camouflage of language: how much, in the attempt to conceal, is revealed. At the briefings, the favoured line was, "Contact was made." Not even, "We/they made contact."

I listen to what Ron says about the Yanks. They were a piss-poor lot, really. Went crashing around like a mob of bulls in a china shop. Sat on their backsides waiting for Sunday dinner to be flown in. Cranberry bloody sauce, mate, in the middle of the jungle. Translated: Ron liked the Yanks; he liked their clumsy bigness. He was happy enough, in his own way, to be there with them.

Ron had only one word for the Vietnamese. All the Aussies did.

In a bar it would be, the noggy waiter. The VC were bloody noggies. It was a nog mine, a nog taxi, a nog ambush. The good guys we had come to save and the bad guys we had come to save them from both went by the same name.

I sat in my room and I tried to think about that.

One night I am giving him a back rub and he says: "I deny everything."

I stare at my hands, in surprise.

He lies still, letting me make my discoveries. (And I think: this desire in me, to find such things in him; how different is that from how he feels, at the well?)

Then he takes me and fucks me in a hard, impassive way I find dazzling.

There was a South Vietnamese military training centre in Vung Tau. Some of the kids there, I decided, must be highly disciplined cadre from the other side.

I considered the phrase, highly disciplined cadre. It suggested a staggering confidence of belief.

In Saigon — this was before Tet — one could pretend that the Vietnamese you came in contact with were pro-U.S. (pro us). In Vungers you just knew it wasn't true. Here were Vietnamese people serving you food, washing your underwear. Just down the road was Hoa Long. And Hoa Long was VC by night and had been for years.

In Vung Tau I thought about that more: a double life.

It is raining. We are in the hotel room. Since Ron was here last, his best mate, Johnno, has been killed by a mine.

Ron stares out at the balcony. He is smoking. He says: "We'd just come out into the rubber. It was lighter, in the rubber."

He says: "Bits of him. Hanging from the trees."

He has never said anything this explicit before.

I look at his grey face, his hunched shoulders.

I go over to him, kiss him, press my breasts against his back. After a while, he is lying down and I am moving on top of him. I feel, as I am doing this, that I have become someone completely ancient.

A woman is pushing her soft body against a man's, trying to make war go away. She is powerful. And ambitious. And definitely pleased with herself.

We'd start off drinking at the Grand, then go on to those makeshift places that had sprung up along the beach front — little round huts, they were. I'd try to get Ron and the others to talk about the war. What about Dak To? (Dak To was where the main U.S. fighting was going on.)

What about it? They spoke of the cricket scores back home.

Sometimes in one of these bars you saw a soldier crying his eyes out. "Ratshit," his mates would say. Then look away.

We are in a bar. It's not long since Ron's best mate, Johnno.

A chap called Ian comes up. He's young and he's really hand-some. Ian starts slapping Ron on the back, in a familiar way that is part friendly, part hostile. "Zip 'em right down the middle, mate," Ian says. "Whaddya say, mate? Zip 'em right down the middle."

He's very drunk.

"Beauty, mate," Ian goes on. "One for you and one for me."

Ron, who's quite a bit older, says, "Take it easy, mate. Just take it easy, eh."

But Ian keeps on keeping on.

"One for you and one for me. What do you say? Ripper, mate."

Ron gets up and punches him in the stomach, hard.

That shuts him up.

I didn't see it as any big deal—Ron's punching him. They were all pretty physical men.

What interested me was what Ian had said.

I'd heard it before.

After the drinking and fucking had been pushed to the limit, and Ron was almost asleep, out of it, he'd mumble, under his breath but loud enough for me to hear: "One for you and one for me."

He could have been back home coaxing his kids to eat up their peas.

But I didn't think so.

Hair brushed, perfume fresh, I open the door, expecting Ron. We are going to the Beachcomber to eat hamburgers and drink that weak Yank beer.

It isn't Ron. It is some other soldier I know vaguely. Awk-ward, not looking at me.

A tunnel, he says. Ron went down the tunnel. Then he says something about what kind of bunker system it was.

I think, quite without anger: The technical details are so terribly important to all of them; why is that?

What was he was doing down a tunnel? Wouldn't he be way too big?

Three column inches on the front page of the *Sydney Morning Herald.* Australian Task Force troops. . . . Operation Dingo. . . . Phuoc Tuy province.

At home, the neighbours will be coming to Shirl's door, carrying food.

Shirl opens the door and the neighbours come in and sit down in the lounge room, feeling slightly elevated, on stage. Shirl is holding up like a trooper. Shirl's the widow.

She has that.

The soldier took me drinking. Some of Ron's mates gathered round.

"Good bloke, Ron," they said. "Good bloke." And drifted off.

They were pissed and miserable and it was just one of those things. They did not, they did not, any of them, say it had been worthwhile.

I walked back to the hotel and the night moved like water.

I had been looking forward to the weight of Ron, upon me.

Nadir

THIS was the Christmas Nixon carpet-bombed Hanoi and I went up to the lake to be with Max.

We are sitting in the house, waiting for the parents.
All along the south side of the house big windows look out to the lake.

They will come in through the front door, on the north side. There are no windows at eye level on that side of the house, just a long clerestory row.

The house itself is one big room. Last summer Paul put the windows in and insulated the place. Installed a fireplace and some space heaters.

The pink insulation, under stapled plastic, is everywhere.

It's like living on a construction site, says Paul, boasting a bit.

It's very cosy, says Max.

Very cosy indeed, I say.

Rosemary gets up and goes to the window, then turns and watches the door.

Rosemary, Paul's wife, teaches art at the school in town. I think of how she claims she is going to carve her family history on the front door. Her's and Paul's.

What about her extramarital affairs, I wonder. A border, perhaps?

And what will she do about her brother?

We listen for the crunch of tires.

We do not talk much.

"In for another ball-freezer," says Max, looking out to the lake.

When I get back to the city, I tell myself, I'll write him a letter. A carefully worded letter.

"What do you bet she'll be wearing a coat of good Republican cloth," Max says.

He's referring to Rosemary's mother. He isn't speaking to the rest of us, not really. He just needs to say it out loud.

Because of the war, Rosemary has not been on speaking terms with her parents. She did, however, go to visit them once, right before she and Paul and Max came to Canada. She took her mother's credit cards and went shopping for the things they'd be needing: blankets, cutlery, stainless steel cookware with copper bottoms. After she'd finished, she left the wallet with its credit cards on a park bench.

For others to share, she said.

Paul's parents, like Rosemary's, support the war. But they keep in touch, sending presents for birthdays, American Thanksgiving, Christmas.

Max's father, who is in the Communist Party, the CPUSA, thinks Max should have gone to prison.

To be in Canada was to be ineffectual, Max's father said.

Nobody is interested in what my father, far away in Australia, thinks about the war.

The parents arrive. They walk in and sit down by the fire.

The mother, all unknowing, heads straight for the chair her son used last. She has the same red hair as Chuck's, but hers is carefully dyed. It curls in towards her neck in a style that reminds me of June Allyson, the fifties film star.

I can see her sitting at a dressing table, looking in a winged mirror. On the dressing table there is a silver brush, comb and mirror set, an anniversary gift from her husband.

The father is more like Rosemary, small and wiry. A pat reversal of genes. No hanky-panky here, folks.

The father is the kind of man I've seen getting on to planes first, travelling first class; the confident, tight-jawed American businessman. He was in the Pacific during World War II. That makes him one of those Yanks my own father so heartily approves of. The Battle of the Coral Sea. But of course you'd be too young to know about that, my father always says.

Chuck's mother and father sit meekly in their chairs and they listen to the story of what happened.

They helped put the bombers into the air.

They betrayed their own son.

I'd come up by train. It was dark when I got on in the city and dark again long before I got off. The train laboured through the canyon and out into sagebrush country, where snow lay like salt on the dry ground.

I swept off the train as theatrically as I could. Max liked to greet me by bending over me and leaning me way back, as in some forties movie. Max had studied theatre arts down in L.A., so this kind of carry-on came easily to him.

Paul was at the station, too.

Paul did the driving. It was twelve miles out to the lake. Over the bridge and up the hill and we were waved over by the Mounties. They were wearing their big caps with furry earmuffs.

One of the Mounties stuck his head in, cap and all, to see if he could get a whiff.

We were clean.

"Doing a brisk trade in drunks," Paul said, after we'd pulled away. "Drunks coming home from their office parties."

"Wouldn't mind one of those hats," said Max. "Very Russian."

None of us drank much. Drinking was what our parents did — the cocktail generation. Drinkers were limited people, weighed down, made dim, confused and finally nasty by all that liquid sloshing around inside them. (Although I did have a bottle of Bristol Cream in my suitcase. For Max and me to share.)

Come summer Max would be back with me in our apartment. He was only up at the lake until break-up. He couldn't leave his political work any longer than that.

He'd be coming back. That's why I didn't move up to the lake. It was for such a short time, as Max said.

"There's something you should know," Max said, as we left the highway and began to lurch along the road to the lake. "Chuck's turned up."

Chuck Keesing. Name right out of a cigarette ad. Chuck, Rosemary's brother. Unlike Paul and Max, who had managed to keep their student deferments going for years, and who had come to Canada days before their pre-induction physicals, Chuck had been drafted. He'd gone AWOL, intending to desert.

His father, with his mother's full support, had phoned the base and told his captain where Chuck was.

Chuck had done time in the stockade.

Waiting to be shipped to Nam, at Ford Ord, Chuck had gone AWOL again. This time, he made sure his parents didn't know anything. He went underground.

But he wrote to his sister, Rosemary. Letters with no return address, signed with the name of their childhood dog. Rosemary didn't have to be told who Rex was, and anyway she recognized the handwriting.

Chuck was in San Francisco, in Denver, in L.A. In San Diego he met a woman, fell in love. Her family were Quakers. She and Chuck moved in together above her father's shoe store.

Through that family Chuck became involved in antiwar politics. He joined the Winter Patriots Organization.

Rosemary showed Max Chuck's letters about joining the Winter Patriots Organization and Max put his arms around her for an awfully long time. Anyone would think that Rosemary had joined the Winter Patriots herself.

It's a play on words, Max explained to me. Thomas Paine spoke of the soldiers who deserted at Valley Forge as "sunshine patriots."

Thomas Paine. Valley Forge.

Americans expected you to know everything.

Chuck had done a lot of things with the Winter Patriots Organization, or the WPO, as Max called it. The WPO had speak-outs where vets described the ghastly things that had happened in Vietnam, and the way their training got them into a head space to butcher.

Rosemary's letters from Chuck were full of this. For Max, especially, who was organizing against the war from outside the country, Chuck's letters became news from the front.

Chuck was an underground fighter in the belly of the beast, Max said.

"What's he doing up here?" I asked.

We had to go extra slow because of the fresh snow. Nearly all the places on this smaller road were summer cottages, deserted now.

Chuck's cover had got blown somehow. There were agents in the WPO, everyone knew that. Sometimes a group had more agents than real members, Max said.

The Quakers helped him out. They got in touch with some peace people in Vancouver. Who drove down to Washington to pick Chuck up. An elderly couple, ever so straight, in a big Detroit gas guzzler. Chuck in the back seat. Gliding up to the border guard.

Where are you from, sir?

Canada.

All Canadian citizens?

Yes, sir.

How long have you been out of the country?

Just down for the day, sir.

Are you bringing anything back? Cigarettes? Tobacco? Alcohol?

No, sir.

And gliding on through.

Illegal still, but out of reach of the FBI.

Chuck had spent the night with that family. Next day they put him on the train.

"Chuck's not in good shape," Max warned, as we stamped up the stairs to the house. "Not what you'd expect."

Chuck was a thin, long, red-haired man. He sat by the fire, rubbing his hands up and down his thighs.

"Did you get the cinnamon sticks?" Rosemary asked Paul.

"They were all out," he said.

"What about the red wine?"

"I forgot."

"You forgot."

"Yep." Not at all repentant, either.

"So much for that," Rosemary said.

She went over to the bedroom corner, behind the makeshift curtain, and began, noisily, to wrap presents. The paper crackled.

Paul sat in the biggest chair by the fire, opposite Chuck.

With fastidious movements of fingers and thumbs, Paul began to roll a few numbers. These he arranged tidily on a small table at his side, much as he had earlier piled wood by the fireplace: ready for the night ahead.

Between Paul and Chuck was Che's blanket. As soon as Che saw Paul settling in, he came to the blanket. Round and round, three times. Then, plop; sigh.

"Such a deep doggy sigh," Paul said, interrupting his joint rolling to caress Che's black head. "Were you bored without me, my precious?" Che leaned his head into Paul's hand. "You and me, babe," Paul told him, in a confidential tone.

Chuck rocked uneasily in his chair.

The Chuck of the letters would have even now been chewing the fat with Max, dissecting Nixon's sordid behaviour.

This Chuck had nothing to say.

Max moved around the room, humming. Hummed his way over to the bedroom corner. Went behind the curtain.

"What's up, kiddo?" he asked. You could hear everything, the curtain made no difference.

"We were going to have a little mulled wine," replied Rosemary. "But now, it seems not."

"A little mulled wine goes a long way," I said, to nobody in particular.

"Rosa want a back rub?" Max asked.

"Rosa want," she said, in a tiny girl voice.

I knew right away.

Rosemary is small and delicate. Although dark rather than fair, she looks like Mia Farrow: waif. When the movie *Rosemary's Baby* came out, Max said, Better not get pregnant, Rosa. Wouldn't want to have to worry about the patter of tiny hooves.

Rosemary does want to get pregnant. She has a short cycle and only one ovary (she had a cyst on the other and they had to take it out). But then you never know, perhaps it is Paul. Perhaps Paul has a low sperm count; he hasn't gone for tests.

Maybe, I think, Rosemary hopes that Max . . .

But Max is a total fusspot. Have you got your gong in? Oh yes, Max always has to know. He takes more interest in that thing than I do myself.

Perhaps that's just with me.

If you went into the bathroom and switched off the light, you could look through the breaks in the plywood into the big room. (They hadn't got the insulation up in the bathroom yet.) Behind the bathroom door there was a stepladder. Once you got up on that you had a really good look. You could see right over the bedroom curtain.

Max and Paul and Rosemary went way back to the old days at UCLA. They'd come to Canada together, the three of them. Driving up the coast, they'd heard that Bobby Kennedy had been assassinated.

Max would go up to Rosemary and Paul, put an arm around each. I really love you guys, he'd say.

But he'd never had sex with Rosemary. Paul couldn't handle it, Max would explain. And add: Between you and me, sweetheart, my good buddy Paul is a bit of a Kingston Trio type. All buttoned up.

So what had changed?

Did Paul know? Surely, he must.

Sooner or later they'd notice how long I was taking. I hurried down the stepladder, flushed the toilet, and left the bathroom.

Paul looked over right away.

"Come and put a record on," he said to me.

He does know, I decided. He's craven, like me.

Paul fiddled with his little pile of joints. Finally he lit one, passed it to Chuck.

Who took a toke and shut his eyes. Eyes still shut, Chuck reached down beside his chair, brought up a bottle. Southern Comfort. He was drinking it straight, but only in tiny, abstemious sips.

Whenever Chuck made any kind of move, I noticed, he rocked himself afterwards, as if he needed to regain his equilibrium.

Chuck's a space case, I thought.

I played the Carly Simon, just released. Carly was standing in front of a bunch of London traffic.

"Looks like Piccadilly," I told Paul.

Max and Rosemary came out from behind the curtain. They stood in front of the fire, warming their bums.

Carly was wearing a dark red top. You could almost see her nipples. Carly's big sensual mouth. You're so vain, she sang. Was she referring to Mick Jagger or Warren Beatty?

Max said it was Beatty.

I knew precisely what Max would like to do with Carly. On the bathroom floor.

Would Paul?

Next Max played the new Bette Midler. We're going to the chapel and we're gonna get married.

"Remember that, Paul?" Rosemary asked.

Rosemary and Paul were childhood sweethearts; they'd met at high school; they'd gone to the senior prom together.

"And we'll never be lonely any more," Rosemary said. "You know we really believed that. Sweet Jesus."

Paul poked at the fire.

"Of course, you were so much older then, you're younger than that now," Paul said. He said this in a mild kind of way that threatened disaster. Not now, but later. It was a line from somewhere. I knew I was supposed to know it.

"Time for the news, folks," Max announced. He switched on the TV and we watched the CBC.

"In the wake of the peace negotiations deadlock, the United States has launched a massive aerial bombardment of North Vietnam. The air offensive, which was first denied then later confirmed by the U.S., is reported to have started Sunday in the Haiphong area and represents the first U.S. military activity north of the twentieth parallel since last October."

Rosemary had begun to hand around mandarins, wrapped in their small pieces of green tissue.

She stopped at this point, with three mandarins still in her lap. Max and Paul were holding their mandarins in their hands, the green tissue still around them.

"In Paris, head of the Hanoi delegation to the Peace Talks, Le Duc Tho, has condemned the raids as 'barbarous.' Meanwhile, President Nixon has said that the bombing will continue until Hanoi agrees to the peace terms."

"That bastard," said Paul.

"That total, utter and complete bastard," said Max.

"Radio Hanoi reports that the bombing has caused the deaths of many hundreds of civilians and the destruction of thousands of dwellings. The U.S. command insists that it is attacking only military targets."

This roused Chuck. "Fuckin' assholes," he said. "Fucking bleeding assholes."

It was one of the two things I ever heard him say.

After the news, we went to bed.

Max's bed was on the opposite side of the room to Paul and Rosemary's corner.

I lay on my side of the bed, as close to the edge as possible. Did Rosemary wait until Paul's snores were genuine? (A wife can tell.) Did she then creep over here, to this bed, to my spot? And lie here? Daring, generous, welcome.

Chuck was still up. You could hear him by the fire, rocking back and forth in his chair, coughing once in a while.

Then he made his way to the bathroom.

Coming out, he tripped over Che's bowls. That seemed to rip something open inside him.

"What the fuck are they doing there?" he yelled. "What are they *doing* there?"

He began to kick the dog dishes, noisy and vicious with his feet.

Rosemary came over, pulling on her dressing gown.

"Just Che's bowls," said Rosemary. "Just the dog food bowls, Chuck."

She was at his side. She was holding him.

Max had got up, too.

"Chuck. It's okay, Chuck. It's all right, honey, everything is all right. That's right, sweetie, come with me. We'll get you into your sleeping bag, okay?"

She was holding Chuck and she was looking over Chuck's shoulder. She was looking over at Max.

I could see her face.

Christmas Eve morning.

We sat in the pale lemon sun and we ate Rosemary's French toast. (Ground cinnamon and walnuts.)

Chuck was still in his sleeping bag, but he was awake. Rosemary took his coffee and French toast and put it on the floor beside him. "Floor service," she said. She poured the maple syrup over the toast. The syrup glistened in the sun.

Max put Van Morrison on the stereo: "Brown Eyed Girl." Max sang along: "Making love in the green grass behind the stadium with you."

Rosemary giggled. A complicit, bragging giggle.

So, I thought, it has been going on since summer.

I took another piece of French toast.

"When that first came out, you know, they wouldn't play it," Max said. "Too explicit. Can you imagine?"

Max was the one doing all the talking.

"Hey, man, remember 'Gloria'?" Max asked. "The strip was really wailing, man." I knew what Max was up to. The summer it was all happening, he'd been there (he'd been there, man). In L.A.

"And her name is," Max went on. "And her name is, G-L-O-R-I-A." Spelling it out, the way Van does.

While Max was hanging out on the strip, where it was all happening, tight-ass Paul was at summer school in Indiana, managing to miss the whole thing.

"Who's the grooviest of us all?" I said, as nastily as I could.

"Time to go for the tree," said Paul, asserting himself. "Is Chuck going to come?" he asked Rosemary, as if Chuck himself wasn't right there, in the sleeping bag.

"Do you want to come, Chuck?" Rosemary asked. She went over to her brother's side, knelt down, spoke to him. "Come on, Chuck," she said. "It'll be fun. You'll enjoy it. You'll see."

Off we went, Paul leading the way, with his chainsaw. We walked up the hill where the power line ran. It had turned perishingly cold, the kind of cold that takes your breath away. February rather than December weather.

I put my scarf around my mouth and nose, pulled my cap way down.

As a boy back in Wisconsin, Paul had been an Eagle Scout. I hurried along, trying to keep up with him. If I walked in Paul's footsteps it made the going easier. But he had such a long stride I couldn't keep up.

I fell back to where Max was.

Unlike Paul, Max was not at his best outdoors. He tended to flail about. Right now he was making things difficult for himself, plunging off the track into deeper drifts of snow.

It could be a perfectly fine sunny day and Max would have trouble finding north, Paul said.

"My feet are turning to ice," I complained.

"Let's wait for Rosemary and Chuck," Max said.

Rosemary and Chuck were way behind, walking much more slowly.

When they finally caught up, I heard Rosemary saying, ". . . you made a woman with breasts and Mom was nervous Dad would see."

The snow was much drier up here than it was down by the lake. But it still held some moisture. Rosemary lay down in it.

"Come on, Chuck," she urged. "Let's make angels. It was you showed me how."

Slowly, Chuck knelt down in the snow. He stopped and appeared confused, as if unsure what was expected of him next. Then he turned around and managed to lie down. He stretched out his arms and began, tentatively, to move them up and down.

Chuck, putting his arms out in the snow, to please his sister. On the last full day of his life.

Christmas morning.

I brought out the Bristol Cream for us all to share. We drank it while we exchanged gifts.

It was a grey day but too cold for snow. After breakfast, the men were going out to the lake. This was Paul's idea. It was something he'd done on Christmas mornings as a child. They'd drive out on the lake, carve a hole, and fish. To keep warm, they'd build a fire.

Max gave me a roach clip he'd made himself.

Paul gave Rosemary a watch. "Oh," she said, looking at it, holding it away from her. "A watch. From my very own husband."

Max poured what was left of the sherry into a flask I'd just given him. It was old, with somebody's initials on it. I had found it in a junk store and had been extremely pleased with it.

"Hope it doesn't taste funny in this thing," Max said, sniffing it.

Paul scooped up a pile of joints and patted them into the pocket of his jacket.

"Okay, kids, let's go," he said.

And they went.

Rosemary and I cooked. From where we were, in the kitchen corner, we could see the three of them. They were small and dark against the grey and white of the day.

I peeled potatoes, chopped carrots, washed Brussels sprouts.

Rosemary did something complicated with red cabbage.

I put the plum pudding on to steam. I'd made it two months before, down in the city, and had moistened it regularly with brandy. It will make a terrific flame, I thought.

Carly Simon sang that sometimes she wished, often she wished, her lover hadn't told her some of the secrets that he had.

"What am I going to do?" Rosemary said suddenly. "About Chuck."

"Do you think he needs to. See someone?" I asked.

"What do you think," she said. It wasn't a question.

"Maybe he could go to the clinic," I said. There was a free clinic in the city, no questions asked.

"He might need something more than a trip to the clinic," she said.

"Maybe we could find him a doctor," I said. "Someone political."

Because, of course, it would all have to be under the table.

"It's a thought," Rosemary said.

"Maybe I could get something lined up when I get back," I said.

But Max was the one who knew everybody. If there was some lefty shrink in town who'd be willing to help Chuck, Max would know.

Boldly, I asked: "Have you talked to Max about Chuck?"

"A little," she said. She began to look embarrassed.

We were both quiet then.

She rubbed the dishcloth up and down the counter.

I remember looking out at the lake just after that. There were only two of them out there. I thought that they looked like figures in a Dutch landscape painting, and that one of them must have gone off behind the bushes to take a leak.

I didn't consider this last thought carefully, or I would have realized that when you're out in the middle of a frozen lake you don't go all the way back to the trees. Especially if you're a man.

Paul and Max both saw him go; they told us.

He'd been standing near the fire, they said, stamping his feet to keep warm. The boots he was wearing were the ones he'd had on when he left San Diego and they were fairly thin. Rosemary had made sure he had gloves and a hat (Paul's old things). But nobody had given a thought to his boots.

Paul and Max had even discussed his leaving. He was walking not towards the house but farther east.

"He's heading for Zandowski's landing," Paul had said. Not only was there a track from Zandowski's to Paul and Rosemary's, but Zandowski was home. The whole family was spending Christmas at the lake because Zandowski, like Paul, had got the place fully winterized last summer.

"He'll be okay," Max had said.

They came home without any fish.

Rosemary kept the food warm in the oven until three in the afternoon. Then we picked at the turkey. The veggies grew cold on the counter.

Paul took the truck out and drove around with Max. After that, we all went out together. By the time we got back it had been dark for hours.

"I think we'd better call the R.C.M.P.," Paul said.

"How will Chuck feel?" Rosemary asked. "Having the pigs set on him."

We got the dope out of the house. We cleared everything out, including the water pipes and my new roach clip. Paul stowed it all in an old cottonwood up the road, well away from the property line.

We didn't say anything to them about Chuck's status. It was normal for a brother to be visiting a sister at Christmas.

They set out at first light: Paul, Max, two or three neighbours, some people from town. The Mounties.

About noon the call came through.

Rosemary phoned Chuck's girlfriend back in San Diego. They were on the phone for a long time.

Up on the bluffs above the lake.

Slipped, fell.

Lying face down on the lake.

No, it would have been the cold.

A neighbour, yes.

In the ambulance it would have been.

Just feel sleepy and pass out.

Yes, I hope so, too.

Something had to be done about the parents.

"They have to know, hon," Paul said. "You have to talk to them sooner or later."

"They can stay at a motel," Rosemary said. "Enough is enough."

The parents are subdued when they are at the house. They see the antiwar posters, the coffee table made from an old door, the beds on the floor, the junk store chairs with their Indian spreads. And say nothing.

But when Rosemary drives them back to the motel, they argue. The parents want to take Chuck's ashes back and put them in the family plot.

"Chuck locked up forever in a plot full of Republicans," she tells us. "He just couldn't bear it. I know."

I become the one who stands at the edge of the circle of grief: I feed the others. Turkey sandwiches, cheese and fruit. Steamed pudding, even. Food that lies neglected on plates and is thrown out after a decent amount of time has gone by.

In the drab, pretend chapel attached to the crematorium there is a service of sorts.

"The lord is my shepherd, my ass," says Rosemary, when it is, at last, over.

We are lying on Paul and Rosemary's bed. Paul, then Rosemary, then Max, then me.

We're toking up, passing the joint silently back and forth. I can feel the bed falling down and down, right through the earth, until it comes out on the other side of the world, in my own country.

There, it is warm. It is summer. A few weeks ago they'd brought home the last of our troops from Vietnam.

In my father's backyard, by the shed, the jacaranda is a leafy world.

You can forget all about the war and just go to the beach.

Paul reaches out and turns on the TV. He moves it round so we can watch the news from the bed.

"U.S. B52 bombers and fighter bombers resumed attacks in the Hanoi and Haiphong areas of North Vietnam Monday after a thirty-six-hour bombing halt for Christmas.

"The U.S. command in Saigon has reported that bombers have blasted the area with more than 1400 strikes. It was the heaviest raid of the war, they reported, heavier than the massive offensive of the previous week.

"According to Radio Hanoi, the attacks began at 9:30 P.M. local time. The radio report said, and I quote: 'The U.S. B52s came in large numbers and from a high night sky dropped carpets of bombs in the middle of Hanoi and immediate suburbs.'"

Rosemary gets up off the bed and goes to the kitchen cupboard where she is keeping Chuck's ashes.

She boils the kettle and steams the label off the package. The label has Chuck's name on it, then the names of the parents, with Paul and Rosemary's address. It is typed with an ancient typewriter, and each line is indented in the old-fashioned way.

Rosemary unwraps the box and, with a soup spoon, ladles the ashes out into four plastic baggies.

The ashes look yellowish, coarse and somewhat greasy (although I don't touch them). There are bits of bone mixed in.

She wraps these baggies in a silk scarf and puts them in her chest of drawers beside the bed.

"Are you sure you want to do this?" Paul asks.

"Quite sure," she replies.

"Put some more logs on the fire," she tells Max. "Lots more."

It has warmed up enough to snow. Now it's coming down in a blizzard.

"The airport will be out of commission," Paul says. "They won't be able to leave from that postage stamp. It'll be closed for days."

He's right, too. Afternoon comes and still the blizzard continues.

"I'll drive them down to the city myself," Paul announces. "Take the four-wheel drive. They can get their flight from there, no sweat."

"Why don't you come too?" Paul says to me. "You want to get back, don't you?"

The next day I drive into town with Paul. Max follows, with Rosemary and Che.

Rosemary gives her mother the package. "He can go home with you now," she says, to her parents.

Her mother takes the ashes. Holds them against her breasts.

"He's quite legal now, Mom."

At lunchtime we stop at a roadside restaurant. It smells of gravy and butter tarts and is overwhelmingly stuffy.

Paul nudges my knee. "Come," he commands.

We go down the hallway and into the men's washroom to do a joint. (We have this theory: it is easier for a woman to plead mistake, causes less ruckus.)

Out the window I can see the back of the Dairy Queen opposite. It has a stack of yellow milk crates by the door. As I watch, a very young man comes out and puts down a saucer of milk for a black cat.

The dope is making me feel tired. Right now, what bed will they be using? Rosemary's or his?

I put my face against the cold, none-too-clean wall.

"Don't fade on me yet, babe," Paul says. He takes my face in his hands and he runs his fingers over my lips. "Many miles to go."

The early dark comes and we drive and we drive, down towards the city. The windshield wipers clear a small space, and the headlights pick up the white stuff, coming at us out of the dark then going swiftly back into the dark again.

When we get into the city and drop the parents off, we'll go back to my apartment.

I wonder what Paul will be like. Will he need coaxing, as Max often does?

Then this happens:

Country Joe and the Fish come on the radio.

Paul begins to sing along. "Come on mothers throughout the land," he sings. He looks over at me and I join in. "Pack your boys off to Vietnam. Come on fathers don't hesitate. . . . Be the first ones on your block to have your boy come home in a box."

After Country Joe is through on the radio, Paul flips it off.

But we continue to sing that song, Paul and I. And singing it we drive on, down into the cold, wet city.

The parents, mute in the back seat.

Behind them, with the suitcases, the surrogate ashes of their son.

Absolute Pardon

N EW YORK, 1974 *Voulez-vous couchez avec moi, ce soir?*
Amy sang. All through the summer when the net was
closing in—so satisfyingly—on Nixon, this song spilled out
of the bars and onto the sidewalks of Christopher Street.

What is that in the singular? I asked Amy.

She was good at languages; she had done her Junior Year
Abroad in Paris. On the *ce soir* Amy did a little hip grind, in
imitation of the men.

Amy was thinner than ever at the end of that summer. I
could see the arches of her hips beneath her cotton shorts. Her
long legs were very pale; she hadn't been in the sun at all. She
was busy every minute of the day, it seemed.

I had to wait and wait to be with her.

For a while I thought everything was going to be as it had
been. Amy and I drank Buds and smoked dope. We laughed.
We danced around the two-room apartment off Christopher
Street, singing *voulez-vous.* We were alone and we were together
and it was sweet.

Then Gene came home.

VANCOUVER, 1974 When I told my boss I was going to New
York via Toronto by bus he said, Write me a piece about it. (I
was just beginning to get work as a regular stringer on one of
Vancouver's two dailies.) We'll run it in the Weekend section,
he said. Keep it light and personal. Personal? You don't really
have to reveal anything of yourself, he said. Just pretend. You
got it, I said.

I did write the piece, featuring a prairie thunderstorm and
an overt drug deal in the Winnipeg bus station. My boss filed
it in the round file and neither of us ever spoke of it again.

My boss's name was Warren Jones and he came from Tasmania. Everyone in the newsroom called him that—Tasmania

—as if it were his name. When I first met him he tried calling me Sydney.

Come off it, I said. They'll be asking about the beaches next.

I've already told them about the beaches, he said. The white sand, the big breakers rolling in, and over you the bright blue sky forever.

Warren had grown up in Queenstown, Tasmania, where it rains all the time.

You bloody great fraud, I said.

On the days I brought my pieces in we'd go for a few beers at the Press Club.

Warren told me about his years on the Melbourne *Age* and his move to London, where he met his Canadian wife. Now his wife had MS and was in a wheelchair.

I told him about Joe and Amy (not all about them).

I shared a house with them, I said. Now Amy has gone to New York and Joe has gone to Toronto. Joe went first, five months ago. Then Amy left two months after that. She's been gone twelve weeks now.

Sounds like you've been counting, Warren said.

The night before I set out on my trip I read my Tarot cards. The final outcome of the matter: the nine of swords. It is night; a woman is sitting up in bed. She is holding her head in her hands. In the air above her are the nine swords. The swords look to me like the louvres on the back verandah of the house I grew up in. The woman's hair is clearly long, but it's hanging down on the far side so you can't see it.

She is, of course, Amy.

Amy on my father's verandah in Sydney. Why did that seem so implausible?

She was from San Antonio, Texas. My Pre-Raphaelite Texan. She had let down her jet black hair for me.

TORONTO, 1974 That asshole Ford had just announced to a booing Veterans of Foreign Wars audience that he was going to declare an amnesty of sorts for war resisters.

It was difficult for Joe to talk of anything other than Ford's amnesty program. When was Ford going to make the official announcement? What exactly would it say? Joe and his comrade, Hugh Davie, had four responses planned to deal with the possible variations. All contrasted the full, free and absolute pardon for that crook Nixon with the punitive terms of the amnesty. All called for a boycott of the program.

Joe smelled of Irish Spring soap. He was warm and big.

It was only after toking up that Joe was prepared to talk about his wife, Amy. When Joe had left for Toronto, his idea was that after a few months Amy would join him. (My idea was that she'd stay in Vancouver.)

But Amy had moved to New York. And she hadn't been up to see him.

Go down there and find out what gives, Joe said to me.

NEW YORK, 1974 Gene is what gives, I told Joe on the telephone. He is also what takes. Amy says they make love every night, for what that's worth.

What does she say the lovemaking's like? Joe demanded, cavalier about long-distance phone calls.

She says it's like meat and potatoes, I replied.

In the somewhat costly silence between New York and Toronto, we both savoured this.

If it's only meat and potatoes surely it won't last.

How can she love him for his meat and potatoes? Joe asked. And what's she gonna do when she needs some crème caramel?

A generous man, Joe.

Amy talked to me about Gene. Gene is tidy (Joe is a slob). Gene does the dishes and lines the cutlery up neatly in the fridge, away from the roaches. Gene is writing an article about the Kronstadt uprising (Joe reads only magazines). Gene can talk about Gramsci, Althusser and Christ knows who.

While Joe was being a dumb shit in the army, Gene was an SDS heavy at Columbia. A red-diaper baby, Gene grew up on first-name terms with the big boys in the Party. Whom he refers to, in a knowing voice: Gus Hall and his tired old Moscow toadies.

All of this, I quickly understand, is powerful stuff. I grew up saying three Hail Marys for the conversion of Russia after every mass. I cannot hope to compete. I didn't link arms with anyone and sing "We Shall Overcome" until I was twenty-seven years old. Rotten little Gene was probably doing it in grade eight.

Amy talked to me about Joe. He's like a big kid, she said. Remember all the fuss about the laundry?

Is Gene good at laundry? I ask.

Amy ignores that; she's still on about Joe. Sometimes I thought I'd die from the dead weight of him, she complains. He'd lie on top of me and almost smother me. And he's so big, as you know.

No problems like that with Gene, I gather.

Each night, I hear them. Meat and potatoes and off to sleep. I lie awake and listen to the sounds of the street life.

To get to the can, I have to walk past where Gene and Amy are sleeping. They are lying together, sheets thrown off in the heat of the night. I am pleased to see how small Gene's cock is. I stand for a moment looking at Amy's thin back, its little procession of bones that lurch slightly (Amy has a moderate case of scoliosis). I would like to kneel beside her and run my fingers up and down those bones.

That would wake Gene up. His hair would stand on end like someone in a comic strip. (I colour his hair some fantastic colour: blue; it would turn bright blue.) It would serve him right, I decide.

Serve her right, too. When you got right down to it.

Admit it:
> *Scratch out her eyes*
> *Hope she dies*

VANCOUVER, 1973 At a house meeting, convened by Amy and attended by the three of us, it was decided that the chores must be divided fairly. Somebody, said Amy, wasn't pulling his weight.

Pulling his pud instead, said Joe. He swung on his chair and laughed.

We drew up a calendar of tasks. Every second week, laundry. Amy would have liked to have gone for every week, because both she and I ran out of underwear. But you take what you can get, she said. With a determined hand, Amy filled in the dates with a red felt pen. She put the calendar on the fridge, where, she said, Joe couldn't miss it. Every second Saturday: Joe—Laundry!!!

Laundry day: Joe trails around the house, collecting stuff. He forgets the bathroom towels and has to be pursued. Amy gives instructions about what can be washed with what. Obediently, Joe makes two piles, puts them into two plastic garbage bags. He collects the detergent, some magazines to read, then gets out the Scotch. This he pours into a thermos, and adds a little coffee. For colour, he says. Rolls a few joints, and he's ready.

You or I may go to the laundromat; Joe is off to a party.

He takes the bus to the laundromat, which is located next to a doughnut factory. While the clothes tumble in the suds, Joe feasts on fresh doughnuts. Drinks. Goes out back and tokes up. Reads magazines. Socializes with the other customers, passes round the thermos. Comes home, often as not, with invitations to here and there.

Even cons me into going with him. I sit beside him while he stuffs both our mouths with fresh doughnuts. (He makes this seem like the meal in the great old movie *Tom Jones*: Tomorrow do thy worst, for I have lived this day.) No matter that he gets the money for the doughnuts out of the communal kitty for groceries. I go down to the drugstore to read my Cosmo horoscope (an important new affair may go badly; I should watch my diet). When I come back, Joe has disappeared. No, there he is. In one of the dryers. Urging me to put in a dime. I won't.

I met Amy when we were both teaching English as a Second Language, on a government project in Vancouver's east end.

I was already employed on the project when Amy came for her interview. (Somebody had dropped out at the last minute.) Amy had been in Sweden with Joe when he first deserted and she had taught English at the Berlitz school there. To the interview, Amy wore a burgundy velvet top with coffee-coloured lace. She sat at the table, talking with the project workers about the Berlitz school in Stockholm.

I could see out the window behind her. It was a grey day but it wasn't raining. I hoped we would hire her. I hoped that very much.

We teach afternoons and evenings. In the afternoons I often don't see her, but in the evenings we have adjacent rooms in a local school. At break, we talk together in the hallway, near the windows.

She talks about politics.

What we need, Amy says, is to place the war within the context of imperialism. She says this in her faintly Texan accent; her hair streams down her back; she lifts her head in a gesture I am coming to recognize.

Take the teamsters' strike down in Chile, Amy says. CIA. The war in Angola. CIA. The thing is to make the connections plain. What's happening in Vietnam isn't happening in isolation, Amy says, emphatically.

Only connect.

I put my arm out along the window, right behind her. If I moved my hand, just so, I would touch her. I could reach up beneath that black hair and feel the back of her neck. I imagine taking her in my arms and dancing down the deserted hallway with her. I would hold her as I had been taught to at my convent school, where, being one of the bigger girls, I danced as the man.

Are you coming to the meeting Saturday night? Amy asks.

Yes, I reply. Wouldn't miss it.

We would dance past the lockers, past the notice boards, past the toilets, down the stairs, past the office, out the front door and away.

The nuns had a woman come in to teach us to dance. You must see yourselves, girls (this woman said) as tigers tiptoeing around the edge of a saucer. *That* is how you learn to tango.

But I never learned, not properly. After a few months, the woman went away and the dancing lessons ceased.

When somebody moved out of the house Amy and Joe were renting, it was Amy who suggested I move in.

Come and live with us, she said, simply. We both want you.

The rest was easy. Three is much more than one more than two, said Joe, happily.

Things are better now you're here with us, Amy told me.

Dear Dad, my letters home said. It has been a very mild winter so far. Recently, I moved in with two friends—hence the address change. They have made me feel very welcome. We all get along *very* well together. They have come up from the States. I teach English with the woman, whose name is Amy. She is from Texas, but she doesn't have that much of an accent. She only moved there when she was a teen-ager. Her husband, Joe, comes from Milwaukee. You have probably heard of it because of the breweries.

I come back from my bath and Amy is standing by the window of her attic room. She is holding Lucycat and she is wearing a ratty old dressing gown she found a few weeks ago at a rummage sale.

Come and look, she says. It's snowing. I'm showing Lucycat what snow looks like.

This is the first snow of the year, in a city where it doesn't snow very often. We look at the flakes falling slantwise in front of the streetlight. Joe is off somewhere. At a meeting. Or perhaps down at the beer parlour, playing pool.

Or perhaps he is off with his other lover. In that case, he'll be gone all night.

Joe has this other lover, a married woman. She lives in the ritzy part of West Vancouver. (One rainy afternoon Joe picked her up at the aquatic centre, downtown.) When her husband is out of town on business, Joe goes over to her place. She never comes here. She phones Joe to let him know the coast is clear.

Standing by the window, beside me, Amy says: He's gone over to West Van for the night.

There are times, I tell myself, when this woman can hear me thinking.

Joe's other lover buys him clothes. Amy and I lie on the bed and watch him trying them on. The polo neck doesn't suit you, Amy says. But the colour is right, I put in. It'll do me just fine, Joe says. He smiles at himself in the mirror. It is the smile of a man who knows: women provide.

I think of Joe's wealthy lover in her fine house, waiting for him. Going to town, buying things to give him. I have taken her call. I have heard her voice, asking for him.

And I am reminded of what thin gruel we can get by on.

I am so thankful to be, just this once, quite marvellously on the inside.

The warm room, wrapped in snow, sails on through the night.

I cannot believe how delightful (how scandalous) my life has become.

I grow obsessed with the details of Amy's life. Amy isn't a true Texan because she was born in Pittsburg. Her father was a corporate businessman for what Amy calls the military industrial complex, but he got laid off. Downwardly mobile, the family moved to San Antonio, where Amy's mother's folks live. Her father went to work selling garden furniture. Her mother did the books.

I need to know more. How old was she when they made the move down to San Antonio? What are her mother's relatives like? How did her father's failure affect the family?

I listen to the way Amy uses words. She has no politics, she says of someone. He has good politics, she says of another.

Very much, oh so very much, I want to have good politics. I listen carefully to find out what having good politics might involve.

I go to the rallies Amy sometimes speaks at (Joe always does). When she addresses a crowd, she lifts her head up and puts her whole body into it. I look at Amy speaking—her eyes big with the adrenalin rush, her mouth intense, mobile—and I feel myself expand. The blood pushes at my skin.

I am huge; I am fluid; I am moving outward, into the world.

I look at Amy speaking and I think of what the poet said: her body thought.

NEW YORK, 1974 Amy says: You're not seriously thinking about going back to Australia and leaving us all, are you?

You left, I say. Joe left. You're the ones who left.

What about Warren? Amy asks.

Warren's just a fill-in, I say. After you went, what was I supposed to do?

I was needed here, Amy says. There has to be a strong voice on the standing committee.

I know, I say. Jesus, I know.

VANCOUVER, 1974 Warren brings over his Joni Mitchell albums. Warren is in love with Joni, would like to rescue her. He stares at the naked Joni. She has her back turned and is looking out at the Pacific. Big yellow taxi came and took away her old man. Warren would have been right there to comfort her, if only he could. This is interesting, I think. His wife, Joni, and me. And what does he think he's rescuing me from?

I've had it up to here with Joni, I tell him, coldly. Can't you find anything else to play?

Warren never stays all night. Around two or three in the morning he gets up and goes home. I listen to him stumbling about, getting his clothes on in the dark so as not to wake me. Oh, what a good boy you are, I say.

He lives with his wife in an apartment on Fourth Avenue. Does she know about me? I ask Warren.

Only in a general kind of way, he says.

I often go by their place on the bus. I can look in and see her in her wheelchair, or in an armchair. She sits in the living room, in front of the sliding glass doors, reading in the good light.

What does she read? I ask Warren.

I don't know, Warren says. Books. Library books.

Which, I tell Amy on the phone, just goes to show how it really is, between them.

Why do you keep on seeing him? Amy asks.

I tell her this: One afternoon Warren takes me driving. We go up to Dunbar, a stuffy middle-class suburb. He parks on a tree-lined street and points out a house a few doors down. A stucco house, built along English lines between the wars. Small rooms, small windows, tight-ass garden. It is his mother-in-law's house. Inside that house, his mother-in-law is dying of old age. When she dies, Warren and his wife will move in.

There it is, he says. Take a good look. There is my future. My fate, if you will.

He leans his head against the steering wheel and looks at me.

They will have to have some special ramps built.

We go back to my apartment and for the first time there is passion between us. I hang on to him and hold him in the name of life's limitations, its terrible disappointments. Surely in the face of these we must comfort one another.

Sounds like you two guys do have something going, Amy says.

Not really, I say.

With Warren, I go to journalists' parties: old-fashioned, drunken, talkative affairs, with only a bit of dope smoking going on out the back. One of the other journalists is an

Australian, too. He works for the wire service, Canadian Press. Warren takes me over to this other journo's place. He lives in West Vancouver in a shed at the bottom of the garden of a big nouveau house owned by a pilot and his lawyer wife. The wife is this guy's lover.

There are the usual jokes about Lady Chatterley and Mellors. Then we talk about home. When are we going back?

Warren thinks we should pack our bags immediately, me and the wire service guy. There's a Labor government in at home and interesting things are—finally—happening.

There is never any serious question of Warren's going home.

I'll miss this place all the same, says the wire service guy. We go out of the shed and lean on the sea wall, which is only about twelve feet from his door. You can hear the waves sucking and sighing. Look at those goldeneyes out there, he says, pointing to a group of ducks sliding up and down in the waves.

Used to be oystercatchers here, he says. Plenty of them.

There's birds back home, too, Warren says.

Ah, yes indeedy, the other guy says. He goes back inside to fetch the Scotch.

I lean on the sea wall and look out. What did he say those ducks were? I ask.

I forget, says Warren.

The evening has hours yet to go. There will be more booze, then we'll order pizza, with elaborate instructions for delivery to the shed. More Scotch, then the wire service guy—totally off his brain by this time—will start in:

The voluptuous tawny hills south of Adelaide, going down towards Victor Harbour.

How he rode his bike from his parents' farm in to school at Strathalbyn, a little country town I'd never heard of until I met him.

The smell of late summer grass.

The way the road turns at the railway crossing.

Magpies singing in the morning sunshine.

Can't get it out of my mind, he says. I try but I just can't.

NEW YORK, 1974 Gene is constantly in the apartment. He is writing his Kronstadt masterpiece on the kitchen table. I cannot be sure of having Amy to myself.

The only time I'm guaranteed is Amy's lunch hour. I go to her office and wait for her there. When she is free—and even this isn't predictable—we rush to the nearest deli.

But our lunches are miserable affairs. I've got Gene on one side of me, pulling, Amy says. And you and Joe on the other.

You know how much I wanted to see you, she says.

I do know, too. I know how she had to scheme and plot to get Gene out of the way, down to Philadelphia, for the first week I was in town.

I knew this would happen, she says, forlornly.

I weep into my sprouts.

The waitress asks companionably, Somebody die?

Amy and Gene come to the Port Authority to see me off. At least it won't be so humid in Toronto, Amy says.

No, nowhere as steamy, I say.

Give Joe my love, she says.

She stands beside Gene to wave me off. Making a statement. A statement I do not want to see.

TORONTO, 1974 Amy's working her butt off, I report to Joe. Gene's not, I add. Gene says that amnesty for war resisters is a liberal issue. (I haven't actually heard Gene say this, but I throw it in for good measure.) Gene's writing an article about Kronstadt, I tell him.

Just what we need, says Joe. Another article about the Kronstadt commune. Or should I say, Kronstadt rebellion? Is this the workers' opposition or are these Mensheviks no longer proletarian fighters? (Joe may read only magazines but he's not entirely clueless.) What can Gene the genius have to say about that?

Don't ask me, I say, satisfied.

What she sees in that little turd I'll never know, says Joe.

New York, I say. She sees New York.

In Joe's own life, things are hopping. The news has broken.

Joe and the others are working eighteen hours a day. We demand universal, unconditional amnesty for all, they tell the reporters. Joe had been in Nam and his friend Hugh had been at the Point. The U.S. media, in particular, lap this up. They make a point of including it, they cannot resist. Joe Florio, Vietnam vet. Hugh Davie, a West Point graduate like his father and grandfather before him.

We're going, you know, Joe tells me. We are in his room, blowing a little dope. It's after one in the morning and he finally has time for me.

I know you're going back, I say.

No, he says. Now. We're going back now.

You can't go back now, I say. When he deserted, the army went nuts and sentenced him to ten years' hard labour.

You can't go back, I repeat. You're a wanted man.

Uh huh, says Joe. If they arrest us, it will make headlines, be a focus for the boycott.

Well. Having dropped that, Joe lights a cigarette.

You know you shouldn't be smoking those things, I say, automatically.

He blows a smoke ring. The ring breaks up and drifts in the room.

What if the cops? Sirens wailing, the cop cars screech to a halt. You're under arrest. Only this isn't some cop show on TV, this is Joe we're talking about here. I am afraid they will beat the daylights out of Joe, out of his generous, affable body.

Just don't let them get their paws on you, I say.

I won't, don't worry, he says.

I don't want to have to visit you in prison, I say.

I don't want to go to jail, he says, matter of fact.

The plan is this: Joe and Hugh Davie will slip across the border and surface, simultaneously, at separate functions. Joe will go to Chicago while the patrician Hugh will surface in Boston.

We're getting Ramsey Clark lined up for Boston, Joe says.

If they aren't arrested right away, they'll go on speaking tours, Joe through the midwest and Hugh on the east coast.

I'm thinking of getting Amy to come on the speaking tour with me, Joe says.

Wives look good in the media, he adds.

Joe Florio, always the optimist.

VANCOUVER, 1975 We were going to go together, Amy and me, to see Joe, in the United States Disciplinary Barracks, Fort Leavenworth, Kansas.

She promised.

But she went with Gene instead. She called me from a phone box on the highway.

Gene and I have been fighting the whole time, she said.

How do you think Joe feels? I asked. Knowing you're there with Gene? How would you like it?

The motel is terrible, she said. You can hear the man next door spitting. Cleaning his teeth.

Why are you telling me these things? I asked.

NEW YORK, 1975 When the war ended, I was in Vancouver, Amy was in New York and Joe was in jail. Amy wrote to tell me about the rally in Central Park. Big balloons, orange, yellow and white, said, "The War Is Over!" Tom Paxton sang a song for the war resisters still in exile.

The day after the rally in Central Park—Amy wrote—an American cargo ship called the *Mayaguez*, sailing in the Gulf of Siam, reported it had been seized by Cambodian forces. The ship's crew were not harmed. In a small boat, flying a white flag, they were taken by Thai fishermen to the destroyer *Wilson*. Despite this, the U.S. carried out air strikes over the Cambodian mainland.

A poll, Amy went on, showed that 79 per cent of the nation approved. The U.S., the pollster concluded, "had not lost its will to resist aggression."

I read this rant about the *Mayaguez*, written in Amy's neat hand.

I thought of Warren's wife in her wheelchair.

I thought of the wire service guy and his tawny hills south of Adelaide.

And I suspected that for Amy, the war might never be over.

VANCOUVER, 1973 In the September of the coup in Chile, the three of us were together. As the fall deepened, stories began to come out about what had happened in the stadium in Santiago. We learned what they did to Victor Jara. Amy told me. They tortured him and then they killed him.

Amy and Joe played their Victor Jara records. Whenever I remember my time with them, I hear Victor Jara's voice filling the house. It was an extraordinary voice, at once gentle and very strong. Velvet, charged with light.

One Saturday evening I was coming up from the basement. I'd been down there changing Lucycat's litter. Joe was coming into the kitchen from the living room, where he'd been watching the news on TV. Amy was in the kitchen, making supper. Homemade pizza, and she made her own dough.

She'd opened the back door to let in some fresh air. The old house had windows that had long since been painted shut. Warmth from the stove condensed on the windows, forming little rivulets of damp.

Amy stood at the door, enjoying a brief dose of the night. For once, it wasn't raining.

Looking out into the night, Amy is singing. *El pueblo unido jamás será vencido.* The people, united, will never be defeated. *El pueblo. Unido. Jamás será vencido.* She calls the phrases out just like on the record, stamping her foot with each phrase (she is wearing boots — they make a good sound on the wooden porch floor). *El pueblo. Unido.*

She is doing this and Joe and I are watching her. She doesn't know we're there. And what I think is this: at this moment I am utterly, totally, happy. It will not last, I know. But for now I am here; I am here, now, and I am complete.

I could see Amy's breath as she sang. It hung in the air.

In the Water,
Like This

A SMALL boat on the open ocean in the tropics at night. The lights from the boat spill out as slivers into the dark of the water. The boat moves, and the lights move, and you are aware of the huge black beyond the lights.

You can feel how soft that blackness is.

Later, there will be a moon.

Paradise, according to popular mediaeval European belief, still exists on earth — in some distant place. Ninth-century maps locate it in China. The Hereford map, from the thirteenth century, shows it as a round island off the coast of India.

We're out at the edge of the Coral Sea.

She gears up and gets into the water first. Jumps in, hanging on to her mask and regulator. I watch her right herself, and see her gloved hand come up. The dive master passes her the housing, with the camera inside.

There's a peppy little current running, so she guides herself on the rope along to the anchor line, to wait for me.

We begin to go down and the water closes over us and I am free.

As far as the normal eye is concerned, we no longer exist.

When we are making our descent she gets tied up in the rope, the one that we use for support against the current when we are entering the water.

Oblivious, she keeps on descending.

And I know her visibility isn't all that good in her mask, and that there isn't much light, but really she should be more careful. I grab her and start unfolding her and I'm right up close to her and I can see her eyes behind that mask, and she's glaring as if I'm interfering, rather than doing her a good turn.

So I give her a pissed-off look right back.

She ignores me as we go down.

We put our flashlights on and they shine green in the water.

People ask me, What was life like before her?

I say it was mainly plain chant, but from time to time, Palestrina.

I did okay. Now and then much more than okay.

Their faces ask me this question. They do not use the words.

Sometimes the beginning of tears will come and stand in their eyes. When there is too much about my life that reminds them of their own.

Last week we were diving on a drop-off, going deep for the soft coral. We came around a corner and suddenly the current was tearing at us. It was one of those sneaky, powerful downward currents, and she was directly below me.

Saucers of her air bubbles were floating up past me as I was going down.

As we were swept down in this current I considered, with a detached curiosity, whether she or I would survive.

On balance I gave myself the better chance.

Then just as suddenly the current subsided and we were out of the worst of it.

Tired and elated, hanging on to some coral. Hard, clumpy brain coral, hanging on like crazy.

She didn't know what I'd been thinking.

She gave the small shoulder dance that we use underwater to communicate excitement.

Things aren't always so easily resolved. At one time we were diving in the waters off the West Coast of Canada. They call it the emerald sea. You hit a hundred feet and the green deepens into black.

We'd found a great bunch of cloud sponges—the size rhododendron bushes get when they're pampered. They were perched on the side of a quiet cliff, the edge of which fell steeply away into the abyss.

We were taking pictures. Cloud sponges, which grow in these still deep waters, can be a hundred years old. When you come upon them in the gloom, they are a dirty cream. But under a strobe light, they are warm, like parchment. Heavy, living parchment. The quillback rockfish lives in these sponges. It's a small fish of a metallic orange colour. With downturned mouth, it patrols the sponge folds.

The aim is to capture the glassy warm cream of the ancient sponge, in the midst of which that orange pouter is giving you a cranky, domestic look.

So we're photographing the cloud sponges and something goes wrong. She loses her mask in the gloom. I can see her eyes saucer big and I know that she is panicking, the fear is upon her.

I can't understand why she's doing this, making a small setback into some massive event.

But she is.

It is an animal fear, the fear of being cornered and trapped in inherently foreign territory.

(The air is full of the wet red soil of the country you are due to leave soon, and now your jeep, improbably, begins to explode.)

Fear is stored deep in blood and tissue and once unleashed sweeps through the body with bullying, staggering strength.

Each of us has our own mantra for the fear.

I don't know what hers is; she won't tell me.

Down among the cloud sponges, I take her hand, stroke her arm, and lead her upward. She is doing nothing for herself, she has shut her eyes and is keeping her eyes shut, she has forgotten everything she has been told to do.

I look around for the mask and see it, slipping away over the edge of the cliff, down and down.

(She says, later, when we can talk, that the moment I touched her, as soon as she felt the pressure from my gloved hand upon her suit, her body decided to put itself in my trust, utterly. Having done that, she says, her heart stopped its wild thumping. Settled right down.)

At about eighty feet light enters the water, and by fifty feet it is quite bright. She begins to take a bit of interest in her own life again. She opens her eyes and looks around. She fins.

You saved my life, she shouts, when we surface, bobbing about in the chop.

Nah, I say. No way.

Because who wants to be responsible for that, who can bear to acknowledge such a burden?

We rest briefly on the surface, then we keep on going, right up into the sky. We are above the grey-green water and its surface is no longer opaque.

See the white anemones with their seductive, vaginal mouths. See the orange sea pens like quills some monk left behind in the mud. Look into the cave where the octopus lives (it stares back with a shy, oblong eye). Find the old grey faces of the wolf eels across the way, their mouths opening and shutting like the gummy geriatrics these two are. See the cloud sponges sitting on the edge of the abyss.

See her mask, falling into the abyssal regions, still falling and falling.

My life with her can be like Beethoven's violin concerto, Nigel playing.

I read her the liner notes.

He wrote it, I tell her, in a state of intense lyric serenity.

He had accepted he was deaf. He had friends.

I told her, I have these two things: water and music.

In love, she assured me, plot is the least of it. Plot, she said, is what comes at the beginning and end. In the middle it is like music, like water, the same themes over and over, corny and classical, revealing themselves: phrases opening up, circling around, rippling away, returning.

Then she said, with churchlike solemnity, all big eyes: Now you have three.

What was it like? she asks. Nosy.

Why were we on that road, why anyone, why me?

I was there. Period.

So I run up phone bills, sit on committees, make speeches, bla bla yawn.

Because I am unable to forget about the soil (wet, red); the metal; the sky (upside-down); the flesh of my body.

Their complete and terrible candour.

She's got lots of friends. There's not just me.

I know she talks to them about us, although I'd rather she didn't.

She makes herself sound heroic. Knows better but can't resist it. She says, "We have to make special arrangements," and even, "You can't possibly know what it's like."

She's proud of me, I'm one of her accomplishments. Like when I'm in the pool, crashing up and down with my own special butterfly stroke.

It's a competition and I'm winning.

I know she will come to me at the end of the pool, holding out a towel. With a buzz all around her.

She'll lean down and whisper something silly and sweet and lewd.

I'll try to see her clearly, but I won't be able to because I'll still have my swim goggles on. Doesn't matter.

There will be bits and pieces missing.

That's true of anyone, I'd say.

She has her own treasure chests. Art history's her latest passion. She points out to me the spiral, the whorl and the vortex on Minoan vases. She shows me the man in a woman's dress, playing the seven-stringed lyre. Shows me the Minoan octopus, its sensitive arms all around the vase.

Not drowning but waving, she says.

I accuse her of sloppy thinking.

One of our stories:

We are in the waters of the Astrolabe Reef, Fiji.

Above us, somebody has speared a fish, and there is blood in the water. And now there are silkies coming towards us.

Silkies are members of the requiem family of sharks.

There are two silkies, thick, ten-foot sleek creatures, drab khaki on top, pale below. Easy swoosh swoosh of the dorsal fin and they are between us, giving us the once-over.

I look at their mouths.

I glance across at her.

She sends me back a hollowed-out, intense stare.

I understand that there is much I have kept hidden from her, which at this moment I would be rashly willing to share.

Later, she maintains there were three sharks: the two big ones and a baby. The little one, she said, followed in the wake of its mother.

She likes to speak of this baby silky shark, the one that never was. Claims it moved its small dorsal fin elegantly, just like the grownups.

Oh yes, I lie, when she tells this story to strangers. There was the baby, too.

I put my hand out along the couch behind her, or touch her leg.

Her mother loved her father. But he came back from the war with head injuries.

Her father: a tall handsome man sitting in his chair on the verandah, in Sydney.

Her father, saying nothing.

Sitting totally still.

She remembers her father lying in his room (her parents had separate rooms). Lying on his bed, with the blinds down, for weeks on end. Shutting out the bright antipodean light.

Those were the bad times.

We're all on tenterhooks, her mother whispered importantly to the parish priest in the front hall.

She thought that it meant "on tiptoe," because this was how her mother walked during these bouts.

In and out of the hushed room. On tenterhooks.

Her mother, who was English, flew back to England. Just the once. Before she went her mother put into the freezer four months' supply of frozen food. On the fridge door her mother left a diagram of what should be thawed and eaten when.

To look at my father, she says, you would have thought there was nothing wrong with him at all.

A tall, handsome man.

A very simple description.

She saved my life, as once she thinks I saved hers.

An afternoon dive, the third of the day, and I'm down at only sixty feet, looking at a lionfish. The head of the lionfish is excessively decorative. Flaps and flags and spikes hanging off all over. The lionfish has long pectoral fins, about a dozen on each side, poisonous. Its body is dark maroon with cream stripes. The stripes go through its eyes as well.

With all that to notice, I had more than enough to be thinking about.

I ran out of air. It's a stupid thing to have to confess, but I'm not always checking to see how much air I've got left.

It was such a mild, easy afternoon that I forgot.

You can go crazy and die down here, no problem. Rapture of the deep. Tee martoonis, glug glug drown.

Sometimes it seems inviting.

If I leave you, she says, or if you die, I'll get my own place with old oak furniture and lavender in pots. I'll buy antique plates that don't match, with flowers on them.

Give me a break, I say.

I'd like to grab her by the hair, bring her face down into mine, scare her good.

I was a soldier boy, you know. One young dumbfuck. Picked up an attitude, you better believe it.

The trouble is, she says, most of the plates you can find cheap, secondhand, are those dreadful ironstone things from the early sixties, with one crude big daisy or sunflower on them.

Just kidding. I'm a man of peace these days. That's my shtick, you might say. My shtick, my stick.

Anyway I can't reach her hair. I'd need to add half a foot to my arm (ha ha).

There's nothing to stop you, I say, from getting some pots of lavender for our place.

She looks at me as if I have missed the point entirely.

Well, to be quite frank, I think about leaving her, too.

Most relationships with someone like me break up. They can't take it, the other party. Because a party it ain't.

I've seen that look on her face: she's hanging on and on for dear life, like grim death. She's polishing up her big fat halo. Hanging in with the ole crip.

I can't tell you how it makes me feel, seeing that look.

I think how peaceful my life would be without her, without her discontent. Without her judgements. (And she's very picky; have I told you how picky she is? Muddy wheel tracks on the carpet drive her crazy.)

But when I'm out of air I'm not planning on leaving her.

Or dying.

Not just yet anyway.

I'm looking around for her, and fast.

She's poking about near some tunicates on the edge of a coral outcrop. Tunicates are little living sacs. These particular tunicates are the size and shape of human hearts. Complete with valves and artery-like openings, they pump water as if it were blood. They are blue and white, exactly like the delftware in my mother's china cabinet.

She's over there by the delftware hearts. Open hearts, throbbing away. (In certain lights they are not blue but purple.)

I swim across to her and make an out-of-air sign: a slashing motion across the throat.

Her body goes still with this news.

Then right away, without any hesitation whatsoever, she takes the regulator out of her own mouth and gives it to me.

I hold on to her.

She's looking pleased with herself, because we're doing this right, and because she's rescuing me.

Slowly, sedately, we rise to the surface: her breath, my breath. Buddy breathing. Her and me, conspiring in the sunshiny water.

I hear her on the phone one day. He's such a baby, she is saying. She's talking about me.

Now there are times I don't mind being her baby, you understand. But not the whole fucking time. Not on the phone, to her friends, who are oh so supportive.

I go into the kitchen and attack the cat food bowls by running my chair over them. The cat, he's supposed to just have Science Diet but he likes that runny stuff.

I roll my wheels in the runny stuff. Then I roll into the living room, round and round. As I do this I'm thinking about how you used to be able to ruin the phone when it was attached to the wall. These days the bloody thing would just pop out of its jack.

He yanked the phone right off the wall. Sounds good, doesn't it? Satisfying.

She has to clean up.

Some things are unforgivable, she says, down on her knees, rubbing at the carpet.

They are, I say. They are.

Like me, she gets bored. I've seen her boredom, although she denies it, later.

She can be swimming about in a coral garden and everything is moving in the water, everything is alive, sucking, swaying. Or just pretending to be dead, all the better to pounce. Here are the fish you've seen in the aquarium, with their peerless, moving colours.

Consider the harlequin tuskfish: body of orange-red stripes. Prominent blue teeth.

She can look at those bright blue teeth and shrug.

Beethoven's violin concerto was played for the first time by his good friend, Franz Clement, in 1806. Between the concerto's first and second movements, Franz tossed in some pieces of his own, including a sonata which he played on one string with his fiddle turned upside-down.

The concerto itself promptly sank into obscurity.

At this moment, on our night dive, she is among the golden sea fans, the gorgonians. I can't see her except when the strobes flash. Then for less than a second I can see the intricate twists of a huge golden sea fan, its irregular, veined beauty. I can see the fan in silhouette, and behind it, the density of her body. Her body, hidden now inside her wetsuit. (You should see her peeling off wetsuit and swimsuit: neck shoulders breasts, like cream, like silk, like this.)

Off to my right a turtle goes by me. Precise little flap flaps putting distance between itself and the ugly foreign thing.

The sea fans are golden only under water. If you bring them to the surface, expose them to air, they turn black, they die.

I'm hanging here in the tropical water, waiting for her.

Right now I'm feeling pretty good. I'm having an excellent day.

My mind keeps chugging along — it's stuffy back in our cabin, I don't know how they can bear to swim among these fish and then eat them for dinner, their rates really are a rip-off, maybe I'll have a Deep Spring orange when we get back to the boat—it's a junkyard in there, the usual.

(You want to know how I get down the narrow stairs into that cabin? Well, I'll tell you: I crawl and haul, folks. A forty-eight-year-old crawler and hauler, very dexterous.)

But out here, in the water everywhere, above and below and within, there is floating and purring and waving and pulsating.

Then there it is—

The flash of light, the moment of illumination.

She is swimming along in front of me and we are making our way back to the boat. We switch off our flashlights and I can see the phosphorescence coming off her. She moves her legs economically, letting her fins do the working.

I swim behind her.

I imagine that my own legs can move. I pretend they are imitating her legs, keeping in time with her.

Synchronicity.

Like the times she dreams my dreams, or tries (like this) to speak my thoughts.

Minute silver flashes of phosphorescence go right around the edges of her body. I hope she doesn't notice them, because she'll pass me the camera and start doing handstands, or waving her arms to swim like a manta ray.

Sometimes she wears me right out.

And all I want is for her to stay like this, moving in the dark waters with me, sparkling.

Flowers for Magda

A *Guernica* of the oceans. That's Magda's next painting. In the lower left-hand corner, the French, blowing up penguin colonies. In the upper right somewhere, the dead seals of the Baltic.

Magda admits the title's in the "some nerve" category. "Just a working title," she says. "A working title is meant to inspire."

Marion isn't listening, not closely. She's thinking about what she's going to do in the garden, after she's cut back the bougainvillea. She's going to put in native shrubs—banksia, grevillea, boronia.

She is imagining the deep bushy scent of brown boronia.

"Don't you think it's a bit obvious?" Marion says.

It's a Saturday morning in October and already it's hot. Yesterday it got up to forty in the western suburbs, an unheard-of temperature for this time of year.

Marion and Magda both have their feet up on spare chairs. They've finished their yogurt and oat bran and in a minute Marion's going to get up to make them fruit toast.

Szena, Magda's white bull terrier, is on another chair, with a good view of the table.

"Trouble is," Magda says, "this thing's going to take me years."

Outside the kitchen window you can see the bougainvillea. The deep purple one, *Spectabilis*. Left to its own devices, Spectabilis would circle the globe, would be a wreath around the centre of the world.

"I've been studying pictures of fish they're finding near sewage outfalls," Magda says. "Odd growths on their bodies."

Magda, Marion says, is a force in nature. When Magda smoked (she doesn't any more) she would inhale and exhale rapidly, her hands weaving about constantly. Holding forth.

She'll be rabbiting on about her painting, on and off, all day long.

Marion thinks of this guy she saw on TV. He served himself a tennis ball and then he raced around to the other side of the net and hit it back again.

Refreshed from breakfast, Magda's Szena charges from room to room, barking. Sending Marion's tomcat, Thunderbolt, into the linen cupboard.

Thunderbolt's green eyes stare out, racking up the debits.

And Marion, in Magda's presence, grows slow and idle and rather solemn.

Eventually Magda says: "But I've been doing all the talking. What about you?"

"Finding you again was a great, good thing," Magda frequently tells Marion.

Marion says: "It was you who went away; I was here all the time."

Last night, Marion asked Magda: "Do you think you've come to, well, fruition?"

For they are, by now, in their late forties. And if not now, then when?

Marion is in the garage, getting the ladder out. Magda and Szena have gone out into the yard with her, to inspect the bougainvillea. It's pushing boisterous, ropy branches up under the roof. Within one week, it has grown more than a foot.

There's no man around the house for the bougainvillea, not since Marion's husband, Bruce.

"Imagine how bored I'd be by now," Marion says.

Later, Marion and Magda will nip down to the shops for the papers and bread rolls. They'll sit in the backyard, under the jacaranda, and read each other tidbits.

In the afternoon they're going up to Waverley cemetery. The cemetery, on a headland overlooking the Pacific, is one of their favourite places, especially in the spring, when the freesias are out.

Magda has almost finished a painting of the place.

When she isn't painting, Magda is campaigning for the south-east forests. The names roll off her tongue — Tantawangalo, Coolangubra. So do the phrases: hydrology of catchments, abundance of wildlife, need for detailed assessment, high value conservation areas.

She speaks softly at first. "Daishowa has been getting chips on the cheap," she explains, in a gentle, factual voice. "Large hollows for the powerful owl and the yellow-tailed black cockatoo only form in trees at 190 to 200 years."

By the end, however, she's right over the top. "You can chop down all the trees in the forest," she shouts, "you can kill all the fish in the ocean, but *you can't eat your money!*"

Yesterday evening they'd ordered pizza, which they'd eaten with champagne. Magda's up from the south coast, where she has a cottage by the sea. At first she shared it with her lover, Diana. But three years ago they broke up; Diana went back to Canada.

It was time, that's all. They'd grown in different directions. (That wasn't what Magda said at first.)

On Monday, Magda's going in for more tests.

"Good champagne," Magda says, "is what made coming back to Australia worthwhile."

Magda always talks as if she'd just got back, although it's going on for six years. It annoys Marion, the way she does that.

Not that she should be being mad at Magda. Not now.

After the champagne Magda did herself as a kid, with her chocolate-thick Hungarian accent, being Buddy Holly: "That'll be the day AY AY that I die."

Having survived being a migrant in Australia in the 1950s, Magda claims, one can survive anything.

"Maybe I'll just get them to take out the whole job lot," Magda says.

When they go to bed, Magda kisses Marion on the cheek. Gathers Szena up and disappears into the spare bedroom.

"Night night, sweetie," Magda calls out.

Marion lies in her bed and waits for Thunderbolt to show up.

"Where's my boy?" she calls quietly.

Hears him pad-padding up the hallway.

Beside the bougainvillea, the frangipani. Standing naked this time of year, thick stems poking up. Right in the heads of the stems, new buds are swelling.

"Boys' school on dance night," Magda says.

Marion's father put in the frangipani. She'd watched him. Marion's father had been in Bougainville during the Second World War. He wrote letters signed, Your loving husband. As a child Marion read all the letters; they were in the back of her mother's underwear drawer.

The chips are high here, her father had written from Bougainville.

That sounded nice. She liked chips.

Her father had worked in a nursery. Because, her mother said, he had no get up and go.

She, Marion Anne Purcell, had loved her father. Who died in 1958, the year Magda arrived. He had died in the springtime of the year, about this time.

Marion's father grew up on the black soil plains near Narribri. The Depression forced him off the land.

He took his daughter back to the property, showed her the endless white sky over the plains.

"That's how a sky should look, princess," he said.

At night they went out, just the two of them, and stared at the Milky Way.

"It makes you wonder," her father said.

"Why didn't you go back, after the war?" Marion asked her father. "Become a soldier settler, get a few acres?"

"After the war," her father said, "there was your mother."

It had been a big funeral, with such a lot of flowers. Her father was buried at Waverley, in his wife's family plot.

Standing by the grave, Marion looked up and saw her friend

Magda. She was at the back of the crowd, her red hair under a black lace mantilla. Magda scarcely knew Marion's father; Magda agreed that Marion's mother was impossible; Magda was there because of her.

These days Marion speculates about other women, single women like herself. No children; unattached.

Marion considers the word, unattached.

Women who have bought houses and settled down on their own.

You see them working in their gardens on summer evenings, and at the weekend.

There is often a cat, a dog.

Is unattached as much a misnomer for them as it is for her?

Back in the sixties, when Magda had her baby just before she left for the States, Marion went to visit.

Magda, caught up in that weightless, expansive euphoria that can follow a birth, lay abed like a diva.

"Laszlo," said Magda, her voice charged with awe. "I'm going to call him baby Laszlo."

"Now there's a good Aussie name," Marion said, and Magda laughed.

Marion's mother had come too, to look at the baby.

"Oh, let me hold him, just a little hold," Marion's mother demanded.

Marion surveyed the scoured bundle that was baby Laszlo. She was not impressed.

The room that day was full of huge blue agapanthus and the airy red Christmas bush. It was December.

Agapanthus and the Christmas bush together in a clear vase. So open, large and light. Generous as summer itself.

If only, Marion thought, vaguely. If only.

Outside, the southerly had arrived, and was attacking the sugar gums.

Canopies of leaves were being buffeted and buffeted.

One of the first paintings Magda did when, in her early forties, she seriously began to paint, was a portrait of Marion.

It isn't a portrait in any strict sense; Marion didn't sit for it.

This is the young Marion. She is wearing a shift dress that is too tight for her, and she will not meet the viewer's gaze. Her face is resentful; her body awkward, at odds.

Behind her, a bare house. In the window of that house, a shadow.

"How do you know what I was like then?" Marion asks. "You were living in the States. It was way back. Before I went to Southeast Asia. Came home, had the abortion, just about croaked."

"I was just guessing," Magda answers.

"That whole saga," Marion says.

"It's all we ever do," Magda says.

"I didn't even like you then," Marion says.

"Tell me about it," Magda says, ironic.

Magda's lover Diana was a bit hard to take, of course, like all North Americans who have gone gaga about Australia.

Might one just possibly conclude, Marion said to Magda, could one perhaps be forgiven for thinking, that Diana had invented the flora and fauna all by herself?

"Isn't it darling!" Diana exclaimed, of everything furred and marsupial.

She wrote a poem cycle about the Sydney red gums, sent it back to Canada where somebody published it.

> Thick-limbed, irregular, twisted pink-oranged bark
> Now newly smooth.
> Your red-tipped leaves
> Rock-clinging roots
> Your creamy flowers your
> Ovoid fruits.

"Oh dear me," said Marion.

"It's a love poem," said Magda. Then shrugged.

Marion laughed.

A few months later, Diana was gone. Marion had Magda all to herself.

They walked by the calm winter ocean, down the south coast.

"My heart is empty," Magda said. "The lights are on but nobody's home."

A friend in need is easy, Marion thought. It's the friend in love that's difficult.

Marion claims she remembers every detail of the year Magda came home. Who played whom in the cricket tests, which side won, who got a century. How there was much media debate about drunkenness on the hill during the one-day matches.

There was an unusual number of dry electrical storms but very little rain. A few of those Royals came out and stood about in big hats while locals curtsied. The garbos threatened to go on strike, then didn't.

It was the year Marion's husband, Bruce, left her.

Came home one day and blurted it out. As if he'd just been to the doctor's and had a disease confirmed. Degenerative, incurable.

He looked anxious, stricken. Beneath that, not quite hidden from her, eager.

A ferrety face, her father would have called it.

"I feel just terrible about this," he kept saying. "Really terrible."

He tiptoed up and stood behind her as she rinsed the dishes.

He spoke of fate. Of the need to be who he really was.

He clutched his stomach and ran to the toilet.

With the habits of marriage, Marion walked to the linen cupboard, took out a clean towel, and went to comfort him.

Throughout that summer, while Magda waited for Diana to arrive, she and Marion drank single malt Magda had bought at the Honolulu Duty Free.

Bruce had packed his things and left.

On the wall, pale shapes where pictures once hung.

For love, Magda explained, Diana was giving up everything. Her home near a park, with its view of the water. A good job in hospital administration. Her husband of twenty-three years. Her two children, their approval. (The boy was a downhill ski racer who nearly made the Canadian Olympic team. The other, the girl — young woman, really — was in second-year med school back east.)

"She feels as if she's jumping off a cliff at the edge of the world," Magda said.

Marion rubbed the side of her whiskey glass, which was sweating in the heat.

They were going to live together, Bruce and his new love, Barbara.

"That's funny," Marion said. "That's exactly how I feel."

Magda told Marion the story of how she met Diana.

It was towards the end of September, Magda said. There's that little bit of a hiatus between the beginning of term and the first round of assignments to grade. In those weeks Magda could sense it; she knew she was going to meet someone and that it was going to be — incalculable. She'd go running and look on the beach, in the rec centre, and wonder if she was there, that person. Which one was she?

"I'd search for her in stores, in the library, at meetings," Magda said.

One day — a Sunday afternoon — she felt drawn to a park by the beach. It was a part of Vancouver she drove through all the time, but where she hardly ever stopped.

"I felt this urge to stop the car and go walking," Magda said.

And the park Magda was drawn to was *two doors away* from where Diana lived.

Magda had sat on the park bench, feeling agitated, full of premonition. The morning fog had burned off. Across the water, ships were being loaded with prairie grain. These ships were painted dark red with a broad rim of black at the top.

They were being loaded from cement silos. Behind them, the mountains. Blue mountains, blue sky, blue water.

"I felt as if I was taking a picture," Magda said, "a terribly important colour photograph. It all had to be in focus, with maximum depth of field."

Two weeks later Magda met her, Diana. She'd been at a doctor's office, reading silly magazines. There was the sound of a car crash.

Magda and Diana, the two waiting patients, moved to the window.

Diana turned, crossed the room, stooped to pick up her purse.

"Is that your car?" Magda had asked Diana.

Diana, flushed from bending over, turned to face her.

"Yes. I'm sorry. Yes," Diana had said.

Magda claims to remember the space, the precise space, into which these words fell.

Magda helped Diana with the details. Drove her home. Beginning of story.

"We just meshed," Magda explained to Marion. Trying to be modest, factual, not to claim too much.

Marion thought about her husband, Bruce, with his new love, Barbara. Perhaps they were meshing, right now.

Marion and Madga developed a routine in which Bruce and Barbara were stranded in the late fifties, about to be married.

"Here she comes, Barbara, the blonde bombshell," Magda said.

"But still a virgin on this her wedding day," said Marion, humming "Here Comes the Bride."

"And waiting by the altar, there he is, the loutish swain," Magda went on. "His hair swimming in California Poppy."

"Do you think she's got her baby-doll pyjamas ruly truly ready?" Marion asked.

"Nylon. Pink nylon," Magda said.

"See-through pink nylon," Marion amended.

"Not really Babs's colour, though," Magda said. "With all that blonde-grey hair."

"Better in baby blue," Marion agreed. "Much better."

Magda and Marion are going up the hill above Bronte Beach, towards Waverley cemetery.

They are taking it slowly, because it's steep and Magda tires easily these days.

It could just be that she's not getting enough exercise.

Marion imagines waking up one day in a world that has no Magda in it.

She is walking along, swinging her arms. (She is in her school uniform, fourteen years old, the year she met Magda.)

Will she move more easily, without the weight of Magda?

What she is most aware of is the vast, empty air.

"You have to keep doing new things," Magda says. "You have to take risks. If your hair turns white, falls out—doesn't matter. You have to not be afraid."

When she returned to Australia, Magda abandoned teaching and moved to the south coast with Diana, to concentrate on her painting.

In her Waverley painting, Magda has painted the row of vaults in the Catholic part of the cemetery. To the left of the vaults, there is a shelter, and beyond them, clearly visible in the painting as it is not in life, the beach. On the beach are brown-breasted women, surfboard riders, beach umbrellas. The air is so festive one thinks at first that the vaults are cabins, such as one sees on a playa, in Europe.

In the shelter, which is perhaps not a shelter after all, it is winter. A woman, with the head of a young girl, but thickening in middle age around the waist and thighs, embraces a cluster of grapes. The grapes hang in the air, aloft of their own accord. Blood oozes from the grapes, staining the woman's coat and dripping onto her boots.

Marion is afraid that Magda's paintings are old-fashioned, decades out of date. Explicit but at the same time too obscure.

These days, Marion believes, you're supposed to be under-stated, nonchalant, sly.

She doesn't tell Magda this, just a little bit of it.

If only Magda wouldn't overdo things. On the path coming down the hill between the graves, Magda has her bull terrier, Szena, riding on a multicoloured skateboard, looking ecstatic.

"Szena has to go," Marion tells Magda. "She's nothing but a distraction."

"No, no, I must have her," Magda says. "I want her."

In the cemetery, they head over to Marion's family plot. They look at the names: Conroy, Ryan, Kelly, O'Molloy, Buckley, O'Donoghue, Purcell.

"My people," Marion says. "Totally screwed up."

"Guilt and repression all day all night Marianne," Magda says.

"No room in the inn for me, thank goodness," Marion says. "Mum got the last spot."

"Did I tell you my son is coming?" Magda says.

She has told Marion this, often. Baby Laszlo, now big Les, had come back to Australia with a degree in business admin-istration. Made a bundle on minerals and real estate in Western Australia in the eighties. Found it necessary to disappear for a time. But now he's coming home again.

"My son the developer," Magda says, and laughs in a painful way.

"Doesn't he know that's all over?" Marion says. "Those days are gone, gone."

"Remember this one?" Magda asks, as they walk up the hill. "92 years: Bowled Out."

Lantana and asparagus fern are starting to creep across the family plot; in a few years, Marion knows, the names will be obliterated. Her father's name. Her mother's name.

"Do you think I should be doing something about that?" Marion asks.

"Nah," Magda says. "Isn't there a caretaker or something?"

"I suspect it's all user pays, these days," Marion says.

"You'd think they'd put them in facing the sea," Magda says. "Give the stiffs the view."

Marion picks away a bit at the asparagus fern. It comes out easily, but will grow back just as fast. The lantana, however, is tough. It hangs on.

These tests Magda's going in for, they can't take too long. Next month she's making a presentation to the Shadow Minister for the Environment. What we are seeking, Magda says, is bipartisan support for our magnificent forest heritage.

"I guess it's not a matter of coming to fruition," Marion says now. "More like just one thing after the other."

They stop at the top of the cemetery and look out over the cliffs.

"I always thought that if push looked like coming to shove," Magda says, "I always counted on having, you know, having someone."

Magda is talking about a lover: wake up in the morning; lie down at night; beside. Your soul's witness.

"Mmmm," says Marion, because she doesn't know what to say. I love you? Or maybe she could make light of it, say, Which in our case we have not got.

"*I* love you," Marion offers.

"Oh, I know you do, love," says Magda, amiably.

Marion comes up behind Magda. Puts her arms around Magda's waist and leans against her.

They stand quite still, looking out to sea.

Listening to Music

As soon as I come in the door, I notice that Johnny has cleaned up. I've not been here before but I can tell. The cat food sits in the middle of the saucer, no crud around the edges.

He's stuck to my routine, I'm happy to see. No regular feeding time. Always have something down in case greedy Gus fancies a snack.

I have become sufficiently a stranger to be someone Johnny tidies up for.

Unless he's changed. Perhaps he now routinely spends Saturdays cleaning house so that on Sundays he can sit in the midst of order, reading a library book which is not overdue. One of his new lovers will be coming over later; they'll do their aerobics together, to a tape. Then they'll eat a little nouvelle cuisine.

I take off my coat and put it in the closet. There is a bright blue parka in there, a woman's. For brisk walks along the dykes?

Dutch immigrants built the dykes here sixty, seventy years ago. Filling in with earth the ancient home of the waterfowl.

As I came over the last bridge on my way here, I looked down to see if the western grebes were back in their usual winter spot. They were. Gliding along, elegant long necks aloft.

"So, when do you go?" Johnny asks.

"Next month, on the eighteenth."

"Found somewhere to live?"

"Claude has got something lined up. Six and a half rooms. Downtown. His sister, Marie-Claire, found it."

"Looking forward to it?" he asks.

"Mixed," I say. "Mixed."

I am moving to Montreal, for a job in which I'll be expected to battle my way around in French.

"I'm not sure how I'll go, having to speak French all the time," I say.

"But Claude will be with you," he says.

"Not at work," I say.

Johnny is my ex. My former husband.

Johnny lives on a houseboat in the Kinley delta. Not a ramshackle old thing under threat of eviction; quite the reverse. This is a fashionable complex. There was an outcry when it was planned. Environmentalists pointed to the irretrievable loss of bird habitat. The farmers were afraid that a bunch of yuppies would move in—they did—and the first thing they'd be yelling about would be the chemicals that are used so extensively throughout the delta.

The houseboaters promised not to complain.

And then there was the uproar about sewage. Were they going to shit right into the river? Turds floating by one's living room? No, no. They were all going to have tertiary treatment —more treatment, in fact, than that used by the locals on land. (So there.)

It was in the papers.

"Johnny's shit will be cleaner than anybody else's in the delta," I told Claude. "And not a squeak from him about the biocides."

We drive past the boathouse complex, Claude and I, going to his favourite wetlands to go birding. "Another monument to bad taste," Claude says, looking at the houseboat complex.

"Hi, Gus," I say, looking over, too. When I left Johnny I left my cat as well. I should have gone back for him later, Claude says.

I am not married to Claude. But I am in love with him.

I am in love with Claude and Claude is in love with nature.

"What do you think?" asks Johnny.

We are sitting in his living room. There are full-length glass doors on three sides of the alcove, all looking out on the water. It is rather like being on a big, low boat. The water, grey and brown, is being blown by the wind.

Johnny says he bought this place for its investment potential. Most of the time he's in the city, at his office.

"We get everything going by," Johnny says.

"Chemicals," I say.

"Seals, ducks," he goes on.

"What kind of ducks?" I ask.

"Don't know," he says. "Just ducks." He smiles.

"How about a little white wine?" he suggests. Which he just happened to have chilled, in the fridge.

"I scarcely drink anything any more," I say. "I'll have some with mineral water. Make that mostly mineral water, mind."

"An excellent Chardonnay," he says. "Australian. In your honour."

All this fuss. I feel uneasy. Really, I should have come with Claude. I asked him to come, but he was busy. (When is he not?)

"You should get some bird books," I tell Johnny. "It's a fantastic opportunity."

Come to think of it, I should have brought over one of the old ID books Claude doesn't use any more. The old Golden edition. Here is Johnny, sitting slap in the middle of some of the most prolific wetlands in the Pacific Northwest.

"So tell me about Montreal," Johnny prompts. "What are you going to be doing there?"

I tell Johnny about my job. Johnny tells me about his. "They're sending me to a conference in D.C. in January," he says. "Giving a paper, as a matter of fact."

"Is that right?"

A few years ago it would have been a training workshop they were sending him to. Now, giving a paper. And is the U.S. military tied up with this conference by any chance? Lurking in the wings, dangling moneybags? Time was when Johnny would not have had anything to do with this dubious research that now pays so handsomely. Time was when Johnny was active on the left. In Red Star Rising.

Red Satyr Rising, Claude says.

Claude had known Johnny in the old days. They all knew each other.

Johnny was the only child of elderly parents. As a child—he told me this, numerous times—he would observe on his parents' faces a look of surprise, followed by defeat. They could not believe what had happened to them. All that lifting and carrying. And when they were so busy with other things.

He had held up his arms and been refused.

When he said that, I thought of a line by Leonard Cohen: They are leaning out for love and they will lean that way forever.

Like any former spouses, Johnny and I sit here chatting on top of an enormous pile of dirt. For example:

In the time I was with Johnny he must have slept with every woman on the left who was willing to give him the time of day. Johnny was notorious. This was the seventies, and as the decade went on and the women's movement gathered strength, he was under more pressure and things were not so easy for him.

One evening Johnny and I were eating at our favourite Chinese restaurant. Great potstickers, and cheap.

A woman we both knew came over to our table.

She'd been sitting with three other women at a table beside the door.

Her name had been Jennifer but she'd changed it to Luna. It made me think of Luna Park, the amusement park in Sydney; but she came from Chicago, this woman, so it wouldn't have meant that to her.

Luna said: "I've been wanting to do this for a long time."

She was nervous.

"I want to give you my anger, Johnny."

Johnny looked startled. We both stopped eating.

Her gums were showing.

"You gave me a lot of pain and I feel a lot of anger," Luna went on. "I'm warning other women about you, so they'll know what you're like."

"Luna, for Christ's sake," I said.

Conversation at the neighbouring tables was coming to an end.

"Let me go on," Luna said. "And you stay out of this. I feel compassion for you," she said to me. "I do, you know. You have your own anger and you must find your own power to confront it."

Compassion. La di dah.

For me. The nerve of her.

Then Luna went on to tell Johnny—and everyone else— how she wished, most sincerely and very much, that she was walking across his face in her hiking boots.

After that she walked out, unsteadily. She tried to slam the door but it swung on its hinges. The waiter moved nervously from table to table.

I laughed. It was at least part panic.

"A Luna eclipse," Johnny said, loudly.

I laughed again.

The women who'd been with Luna at the table by the door got up and left, too. Giving Johnny looks as they went.

But in the end (I told Claude this, later) I could not stand it any longer. When he came home with the sex of other women still on him, I could not go on. I left in a hurry.

Once I'd finally made up my mind I could not wait to be gone.

"How's Claude?" Johnny asks.

"Fine," I say. "Claude's fine. Right now he's working round the clock on the Kinley Action Coalition."

At its source, Kinley is a pristine watershed high in the mountains northeast of the city. Threatened by logging.

These days Johnny finds it difficult to remember about watersheds, pristine or otherwise. I mean, you turn on the tap and there it is, right?

"You've heard of the coalition, I suppose?"

"Of course I have," he says. "It's been on the news."

Now he's offended a little. Good.

It wasn't quite like that: the villain, the victim. "The sex of other women still on him" is an exaggeration. All I ever smelt was perfume and dope.

And I was a protagonist as well. Bringing men home, sleeping with them. In our bed. For revenge.

I'm forty-six, so that would make Johnny fifty this year. My old man, I called him. Still looking good, though. Grey hair becomes him.

Well, at least it hasn't all fallen out.

A great blue heron flaps slowly by the alcove, lands on the far shore and folds its wings, precisely. "Look at that," I say.

Johnny looks, obediently. "A great blue heron," I say. Surely he must know herons, at least.

"You really should go to the sanctuary," I say.

The bird sanctuary is about a mile from where we're sitting. "There are three black-crowned herons there, at the Sullivan Slough. At the very tip of their northern range."

Claude showed them to me: the two adults, dark backs, all white below. And the little one, strongly streaked in grey-brown and white, not looking like theirs at all, but perfectly camouflaged.

Crypsis, Claude calls it, introducing me to a zoologist's word. Crypsis: the art of concealment.

Claude, down on his knees in the wet grass at Sullivan Slough, peering into his scope, breathing in quick short breaths. "Looks more like a baby bittern," he whispered. For two years, Claude told me, the adults had been coming to this spot. This year they'd bred successfully. "Oh baby, just look at you," Claude murmured into his scope. He clenched his fist and punched the air in a victory gesture stolen from Jimmy Connors, the tennis player.

Now here's where I put my foot in it. I should know better; I have known better.

I do my heron imitation for Johnny. I push my hair into disarray at the back, I hunch my shoulders, I crouch in my chair. Johnny laughs. Why am I doing this? I ask myself.

"Not as good as your sphinx," Johnny says.

That's why.

When I did my sphinx, Johnny would say: "A perfectly adequate sphinx ruined by a perfectly lovely pair of breasts." And reach out.

Johnny reaches over and takes my arm. Briefly.

"Where's Gus?" I ask. "I want to see Gus."

Gus, the houseboat cat, to the rescue.

"Upstairs," says Johnny. "Sleeping, I guess. What else?"

I couldn't take Gus when I left. The only apartment I could find in a hurry had a no-pets policy.

Gus is curled up in the middle of the bed. As soon as I touch him he starts up his motor. Stretches, lets me kiss his belly.

"Fourteen," says Johnny. "Still just a kitten."

"What does he think of the water?" I ask.

"He watches it," Johnny says. "He likes it."

Gus rolls himself up. That's quite enough, thank you.

"The old motor's still turning over," I say.

"He's my big old baby," Johnny says. Then he puts his arm around my waist.

"Mistake," I say.

He takes his arm away.

The day I left Johnny it wasn't raining in the mild, chronic way of winters on the coast. It was pouring on down. I was tired, I was wet, I was fed up, I was afraid. On my last trip out the door (carrying my share of the mops and brooms), Johnny stood at the top of the steps and said, "I hope you find whatever it is you're looking for, baby."

"Let's go down," I say. "Get that stuff out of the car."

That's what I really came for. Claude and I have been cleaning out the apartment, getting it ready to sublet. There is junk there we've never used, some of it left over from my marriage to Johnny. "Maybe we could give some of this crap back," Claude suggested.

Claude hates to waste things. Claude believes in a conserver society.

I'd phoned Johnny, got him on his car phone. "He does want that rug back," I reported to Claude. "And he'd quite like the Coleman stove, the big old one."

"Maybe one of his new women is into car camping," Claude said. "He'd better watch it." Claude knew about Luna's hiking boots.

Johnny and I lug the stuff in.

"Remember this?" Johnny asks. He holds up a bedspread we bought in Greece.

We got around in those days; no money, but we travelled. The trip on the freighter, the nights under the stars—exhilarating, especially in retrospect. We even brought things home.

Johnny had no way of knowing this in advance, but I have come at the worst possible time. For a few days immediately before my period I shouldn't allow myself to leave the apartment. All I can see are people in offices, people walking to the train, people sitting in lighted windows. And none of them is making love. What are they waiting for? Don't they know how short time has grown?

This may be the approach of menopause, I tell myself—the almost exhausted egg supply giving one final furious nudge.

As I said, Johnny had no way of knowing this in advance. But he sure as hell knows it now. Johnny can pick up on this kind of thing light years away.

"I really should be going," I say.

At this he looks so unnerved I immediately feel better. He's getting old, I think. His face is beginning to sag. He's got those loose little jowls on the sides of his cheeks.

"You can't go yet," he says. (Oh, can't I just.) "I've something I want you to hear. DDD makes all the difference." He holds up Mahler's Fifth, by the conductor we agreed was the best— slow and sensual and precise. "Wouldn't you like to hear this?"

"At least listen to the third movement before you go rushing off."

The music unfolds slowly, taking its time. *Mit Warme.*

Claude is so busy these days, working on the Kinley coalition. No doubt there will be something else when we get to Quebec. This planet is choking on human shit, Claude says. He'll find something to hone in on in no time at all.

In the old days Claude called himself an anarchist. Now he calls himself a Left Green.

For years I used to see him at rallies and benefits, wearing his black-and-red scarf. I remember thinking that it made him look like a big boy scout.

Claude has a couple of degrees in zoology, but he works at a local independent cinema. Sells tickets, serves popcorn, sweeps up after everyone has gone home. That way he makes enough to pay for groceries and rent. He can keep his real self, the creative part, for his environmental work.

One evening I was at the cinema, getting a coffee at interval. It is the kind of cinema that sells not only popcorn but coffee, fruit juices and health bars; it is the kind of cinema where you can see two in a row for the price of one. I noticed Claude watching me. He was serving someone else popcorn at the time, but his body — I could tell — was alert because of my proximity. Under that awareness my own body grew discrete, detached itself from its surroundings.

I stood out in sharp relief; I was the only other person in the foyer.

It made me short of breath.

Not this again, I thought. Lord, *this* again.

The violins are starting to make their claim. Falteringly at first, but gathering ambition as they go. Higher, higher. They are on their way.

The harp, far above it all, waits.

There was a night once, with Johnny, when after much arguing and dope smoking and lovemaking, we watched the dawn and listened to Mahler's Fifth. And I said, "The harp always makes me tense. I know it is a message straight from heaven."

Johnny said: "Adolescent romantic, that's my girl."

About hell and purgatory—I told Johnny—the nuns who taught me had buckets of information, all in terms of the body's experiences. It was freezing cold; it was boiling hot. But when it came to happiness, they could not make it compelling.

There it was, heaven, a featureless plain. Believe in that.

They had no words. "And you know why?" I said to Johnny.

"Sure I know why," Johnny answered.

He was massaging my vertebrae, one by one. He was very good at that, Johnny.

Outside, the birds were beginning to stir.

Moving above the violins, the celestial harp. Dirk Bogarde in Venice, the hair dye running down his face; the young Tadzio in his sailor's suit. How beautiful they both were: Dirk and Tadzio. Because it does not last, it does not last nearly long enough, and how they know it—Mahler, Mann, and Visconti, too, Johnny said.

I remember Johnny. Now, Claude.

With Johnny, as with the others, the body remembers. Johnny was much more of a pony than Claude; he liked to leap about. Johnny had read somewhere that vigorous move-ment can give a man more of an all-over orgasm, like a woman's.

Poor Johnny, striving for what he cannot reach.

In Johnny's eyes, a genuine relationship acknowledged that after three years or so (Johnny gave it three years, max) the bloom dies. This does not mean you break up, not necessarily. You can go on together, if you wish, bound by the thousand other things.

But you seek the yearning, the bloom, elsewhere.

They climb and they climb, those violins.

I began to go to the cinema at closing time, waiting until Claude had swept out the dusty place. He liked to sit in the dark when he'd finished and smoke a joint or two before he went home.

The empty cinema, with all its many seats, was where we told each other our stories.

Once, I told Claude, when I was with Johnny and things were bad, we drove down to Santa Cruz and stayed in a motel right on the beach. It was the middle of winter. A few doors down from the motel, also facing the beach, was a deserted amusement park.

Johnny and I walked on the empty beach in front of this silent amusement park. We walked along drinking tequila sunrises out of cans and quarrelling.

And I was—sad, sad.

But Claude wasn't like Johnny, not in the least. He had a good reputation. By the time I got together with Claude, I'd become involved in the women's movement. I put the word out on Claude and nobody could come up with anything much.

It turned out that he hadn't had much experience, really, with this kind of thing.

But now that he had me, he thrived. He stopped wearing old jeans that drifted from waist to ass to knee in a careless way. His hair and eyes shone like one of those glossy fur-bearing animals he was so intent on protecting.

I was happy with Claude. I saw him late at night and sometimes, when he wasn't busy, at the weekends. The rest of my life went better because I knew I had the pleasure of Claude, waiting for me.

After about seven months of this, everything changed.

I fell in love with Claude.

The whole shebang.

There was no longer just Claude and myself. There was now this third thing, my being-in-love. It stood in the room like a pillar of light, unnerving us both. No longer was my life made easier by having him (what a distant notion that seemed). Now, instead of content there was — on my part — sighs and reproaches, accusations about the denial of time and spirit. And from him there was a drawing back, a determination to get on with his work despite this.

Yet he was not lacking in courage, Claude. He was fond of me and he was determined to stick it out. That summer he took me home with him. All the way home, to the family farm in the Gaspé. To meet his parents, who lived on the farm still.

I sat at their table and I slept in their bed and I looked at Claude's parents, saw their diffidence and their dismay.

His parents sat on the sofa and watched TV. Claude sat beside them and they talked in the idiomatic Quebec French I could not hope to follow (how on earth am I going to get by in Montreal? I must be nuts).

Claude sat with his parents and they talked about the things they'd shared before any of this had happened, before Claude had gone away from them and become a stranger.

At night he came down the hall and into my room to make anxious, wordless love.

The violins are still heading for the lofty territory of the harp. Up and up they go; they almost make it.

Then they collapse. Glissando.

What a falling away it is, what a long, long journey down.

The moon shone in my room at Claude's parents' home. It shone on Claude's back and ass. It was the height of summer, even a sheet was too much.

On the wall of this room there was a picture of the Shroud of Turin. A miraculous image, it was said, of Christ as he lay in his tomb.

When I was at high school, the local church installed an image of the Shroud of Turin. It was like a photograph in negative. You could look at the face of Christ. He was not in good shape: scourged, crowned with thorns, then crucified.

The real miracle of the Shroud of Turin, my father said, was not that the body of Christ had imprinted itself upon the winding sheet, but that the old sheet itself had managed to turn up in Turin.

I looked at Claude, at the moonlight on his body.

Claude has the kind of ass — compact, elegant, perfect — that could float right up to heaven. I reached over and rubbed my hands across it.

"Quit it," Claude hissed. "You're tickling me."

When the violins fall away, the harp remains unperturbed. Alone in its heaven, in its song. It is moving as it did before, on its own path, talking to itself simply because there is nothing else up there.

I lay beside Claude in his parents' home and reminded myself I would never get all I want from him.

I want to be able to say with truth, I know this man.

Is that an arrogant thing to want? Overly ambitious?

It is what I want.

And I learned much from the visit. I have seen his parents, and that is central. I now can picture Claude, thirteen years old, out in the icy fields of spring, searching for returning birds.

"When I look at birds," Claude tells me. "When I look at them and they sing, their whole being sings, it is — freefall. There is nothing between me and the bird. Nothing at all. Do you know what I'm talking about?"

I know he isn't talking about binoculars, or the rain in his eyes.

When I fell for Claude, when I fell in love with him, the visits with Johnny stopped.

I went over to Johnny's place to tell him.

It was Halloween. Johnny thought I must be some kid on a sugar high and didn't answer the door for the longest time.

I stood in the cold, feeling the sharpness of the air, enjoying the jack-o'-lanterns in the windows and on the porches. And I thought: we know that ahead lies the dreariness of winter, yet still we embrace the beginning of it with enthusiasm.

I followed Johnny into the kitchen. I told him my news.

I felt the strangeness, the marvel of it, coming off my body and moving in the room. He felt it, too.

He leaned against the fridge, holding a beer.

"Well, what do you know," Johnny said. "This girl's in love again."

When we move to Montreal, Claude will have more time for me. He won't immediately have all his days filled. I'll come home from work and there he'll be, waiting for me. The job —the public reason for moving—is the least of it.

He is not as pleased to be going as I pretend he is. But, as I tell him, we'll get a place in the country. After a few months, when we've settled in. The rents back there are supposed to be so much cheaper. We'll get a place by a lake, but in travelling distance of the city, because of my job.

"A motorboat lake," Claude says.

The violins never do make a run for it again. Having fallen from the heights, there is still sweetness, ripe sustaining sweetness. But the grand attempt is over. (Tadzio is gone from the beach.)

There is still the theme, though, they still have that.

Johnny often spoke of Mahler, with approval, as being a man of torrid affairs, scandals, elopements abandoned at the last minute. He neglected to mention Baron von Weber, husband of Maria. As a result of Maria's affair with Mahler, von Weber had a prolonged nervous breakdown.

"What about the baron?" I asked. (I'd been reading up.)

"These things happen," Johnny said.

I had wanted to hit him, then.

When I left Johnny, when I walked out in the rain, speaking the well-worn lines of the defeated (Why don't you just go fuck yourself), everyone, it seemed, was waiting to applaud. Women I hardly knew came up to me and said, I'm glad to hear you've left Johnny, that creep, that jerk, that crumb bum.

It was May Day. Big day for the Left. Somebody who had actually been in the stadium in Santiago in 1973 was talking about the Chilean struggle. And right in the middle of this—

who knows what terrible things this man had seen—a woman comes up to me and says, "Congratulations. Throwing Johnny out on his ear was the best thing you could have done for yourself."

Who were they, these women, I wondered. Had they all known Johnny intimately? Had he been that busy?

I hadn't thrown him out; I'd left myself.

But the women smiled. They were approving. I needed friends.

"Thank you," I said.

Today, I know I am attractive to Johnny. Mahler died at fifty, I think. Or perhaps it was fifty-one. Either way, that would give Johnny a year or two at most.

The music is almost over. The harp plucks away; the theme limps along until it is exhausted; it has no more to say. What kind of an ending is that?

Today, I am especially attractive to Johnny because I am leaving. I am, therefore, without consequences.

Johnny's idea of heaven: an international airport, where every woman is wildly attracted to him. These women are leaving, twenty-four hours a day.

The harp and the violins never did meet; there was no real accompaniment.

It would be easy enough—and certainly generous—to go over to Johnny's chair, and slide with him to the floor. Rocking perhaps a little on the swell of the incoming tide.

In the river, the seals are making their way downstream to the island where they haul out for the night. What do they feel, the seals, as they swim by in the dark green gloom, and see these new hulks?

Perhaps it would stagger Claude a little, if I did this. (If I told him.) But I'm not sure it would reach his spirit, his truth.

Claude's truth has feathers. It flies.

The heron is still over there on the far shore. But it is almost dark now and the bird is difficult to see, it blends in so well.

Learning Welsh

T HERE are moments in August when the wind comes in from the west, bringing with it the cold dust off the plains. Today such a wind is blowing across the town and into the convent yard, where it seethes around the laundry block and catches at the pieces of nuns' attire, starched and stretched out on low platforms by the tanks.

It nibbles at the little cuffs worn by postulants, then it takes on the guimpes, the big bibs worn by the nuns.

For a moment, the wind dies down.

Now it's back.

This time, a willy-willy, a small dust storm, is making straight for the platforms. It scoops up the cuffs and the guimpes. It carries them away, across the yard, over the fence, over the roof of the presbytery next door, right over to the park on the other side of the road.

Where it dumps them.

I see all this and so does Sister Winifred. So do Maria Dwyer and Rita O'Toole.

We are having our English honours class in the sun, behind the hedge.

We are all very senior girls, most responsible.

Sister Winifred looks around the yard, a small, hopeful glance. Some other nun, surely, has seen the willy-willy lift up the intimate pieces of clothing and carry them off to the public world?

But there is no one in sight.

Something will have to be done.

You can't leave nuns' clothing lying around in the town's central park, there to become objects of scorn and wonder to passing nonbelievers. This is a university town; nonbelievers are everywhere.

Her face, bright pink, is looking into mine.

I am unable to move, totally at a loss.

But Maria Dwyer and Rita O'Toole are on their feet.

"I'll go, Sister," they say, in turn. "I'll go." "I'll go."

Off they dash, not even stopping to fetch their hats and gloves, although nobody leaves St. Angela's grounds without hats and gloves, not ever.

This is the first time I have been alone with her since I made my move.

I look at Sister Winifred. She looks at me. Dust blows into our faces.

Did it really happen like this or do I exaggerate?

This is the image: the willy-willy is whisking away the mediaeval clothes and Sister Winifred and I are face to face.

This is the emotion that accompanies the image: it is as if, in a dream, I am walking naked down the street. The same trapped humiliation.

———

Sister Winifred has a university degree—a most unusual thing, amongst our nuns. She is tremendously overworked. On Saturday nights, when we have films in the rec hall, she huddles by the projector, correcting papers in the dim light.

I think she is too earnest.

Yet here it is: I am craning my neck for a glimpse of Sister Winifred's face as she comes back from communion (a voyeur of the holy, intimate moment). I am careful to arrive at Latin class early, so that I can sit at the top of the table. That way, when she has to move her arms to write on the blackboard, I can look up under her guimpe.

If I'm lucky I get a glimpse of her neck, naked and interesting.

I can also see, tucked up under her guimpe, a pocket where she keeps her fountain pen and pencils. And her act beads. Act beads are little beads, usually half a dozen, which you can push up and down. You push one up when you've committed an act. An act is something you don't like doing, but you do it and you offer it up.

Latin is at eight-thirty in the morning. By that time Sister Winifred has already notched up two beads.

What has she forced herself to do?

There are lots of things one can offer up, she tells us. You can put salt on your jam all through Lent.

She doesn't come from round here. If she did, I'd know what her real name had been before she entered. Lots of the nuns are Old Girls of St. Angela's. Some have sisters at school. Rita O'Toole's sister is a nun. In real life she was Eileen O'Toole. Rita is going to enter the Angelines, too.

To know the real name of a nun—we all want this.

I make inquiries about her, but nobody knows. Some say she comes from Queensland and went to the convent at Brisbane. Some say she comes from down the coast, dairy country. That her father is a grocer, a farmer, a doctor.

At least I can look up Saint Winifred. Patron saint of the Welsh.

Saint Winifred was a seventh-century Welsh virgin. The son of a neighbouring prince wanted to marry her, but she had dedicated herself to the bridegroom of her soul. Enraged at being turned down, the prince pursued her as she fled for sanctuary. He caught her and chopped off her head. At the point where her head touched the ground, a fountain sprang up. A spring of sweet water.

Sister Winifred would not have chosen this name. When she became a nun, the name was given to her. She herself would have heard it for the first time during the dedication ceremony.

In our English honours class, we are specializing in Gerard Manley Hopkins. Maria Dwyer and Rita O'Toole are keeping notes. Inscape, they write. Duns Scotus, they write. How do you spell that? Maria Dwyer wants to know. She really is a dunce, she'll be lucky to get a pass, much less honours.

I'm not taking notes. (All that stuff is in the introduction to the book.) I'm waiting for Sister Winifred to read out loud.

I'm waiting to see her face go open and serious as she reads "The Windhover." When she reads she is, I know, speaking only to me.

Maria Dwyer and Rita O'Toole are just along as chaperones.

"He didn't write a word for seven years," Sister Winifred explains. "He was a poet before he joined the Jesuits. But when he was in the seminary he gave it all up. Then his rector said that he could write again and 'The Wreck of the Deutschland' came bursting out of him."

"It was," she said, "as if all that poetry had been building up inside of him, under such tremendous pressure."

"Like oil," I say.

"Yes, yes," she says, relieved. "Like oil."

And smiles.

At me.

Maria Dwyer can't stand Hopkins. "What's that wreck thing supposed to be about? A bunch of nuns going down in the drink?"

Maria acts as if this were a great joke.

Maria says: "When Winnie gets going on that stuff it's like she's taking off all her clothes in front of us."

She makes me anxious, Maria Dwyer.

Sister Winifred's face has become daring and determined, like somebody about to dive off the high board (or at least this is how I imagine they'd look; you can't see their faces, way up there).

"Blue-bleak embers," she says. She has committed herself now, she looks a little desperate. "Fall, gall themselves, and gash gold-vermilion."

Ever so quietly, Maria Dwyer sniggers.

In Latin class, I get Maria Dwyer's basic exercises by mistake.

Maria Dwyer has taken the sentence, The boy who loves

the master is good, and translated it as, *Puer, quem magister amat, bonus est.* Which means, The boy, whom the master loves, is good.

Trust Maria Dwyer to get it back to front.

Sister Winifred has corrected it. In the margin, she has written, for Maria Dwyer's instruction: *Quem*—accusative as obj. to *amat.*

She even fixes it for her: *qui magistrum.*

Not that that will do dim Dwyer any good.

"He was in a seminary in the Welsh hills," Sister Winifred says. "Studying theology. He wanted to learn Welsh, he was drawn to the music of it. But the rector said he could not approve unless it was for the purpose of labouring among the Welsh, to convert them."

As she is saying this, I am watching her hands. She doesn't use any hand cream, of course. Her hands are cracked and dry and there are fine residues of chalk sitting in the lines.

"But it wasn't, you see. It was for the poetry."

Now she is looking right at me.

"Maybe Welsh could have made his poetry better," I say. "And if his poetry was for the greater glory of God. . ." I trail off.

"Do you think it was the wrong decision?" Sister Winifred asks me. I can feel some need coming from her.

"The poetry is what survived," I argue.

I am into this now, I have to keep going. "It serves the greater glory of God even though Hopkins himself is long dead."

(Where did that come from? I am out of my depth.)

"But the rector said," she replies.

With this, I feel her going away from me. Literally, I see her shrink back into her habit.

I understand what she means: the vow of obedience, the chain of command. If the rector decrees that black is white, so be it.

I do not accept.

"He should have learned Welsh," I insist. "He should have."

I am horrified to hear my voice as it comes out. Shaking, near tears.

I become more critical of her, more nervous.

At benediction I cry into my mantilla. I keep my head bowed, and hope nobody can see. I believe I am weeping for Hopkins, the poet, denied his opportunity to learn the lovely language of Welsh.

He was sent to a parish in Liverpool, in an industrial area, a poor district.

I see him walking down the street in his soutane—timid, frail, with soft skin that never sees the sun. He comes to a smithy's. The fire burns and the big smithy raises those powerful arms and the horses stand in massive nakedness.

We have a grey draughthorse at home on the property. He doesn't work any more. Now we use the Ferguson tractor. He lives in the house paddock, this big horse, gone at the knees.

"Somebody should send him on his way," my brother says, fooling around. "Off to the knackers. Glue, anyone?"

"Leave him be," my father says.

I watch my father go over to him, sink his head into the horse's neck. My father puts his arms around the old horse and caresses him.

"Stupid old sook," my brother says, embarrassed.

Something happens. Rita O'Toole's sister is moved to our convent. On visiting Sundays Rita is allowed to sit in the front parlour with her sister, Sister Ambrose, who tells her this: she was a postulant with Sister Winifred.

Postulants tell each other everything, Rita O'Toole says, happily. Rita has a vocation, she can't wait.

Sister Winifred entered the convent, Sister Ambrose says, because of the Kempsey floods.

She was home from uni, and looking after a neighbour's family. The mother had just had another baby and wasn't well. So Sister Winifred, not yet a Sister, whose real name is

Gertrude, goes to the farm to help out. Takes care of the baby, feeds the kids, so the mother can get better.

Down comes the flood, one of those huge floods of the early fifties that took all before them.

The mother and the kids drive out in the Dodge. Sister Winifred is following in her father's Austin, with the crib in the back. (There are so many kids there's not enough room in the Dodge.)

The mum and kids get out okay, but when Sister Winifred is driving the Austin through the last creek, she is swept away. The car sinks.

Sister Winifred escapes. Ends up high in a gum tree, clutching the baby and watching the water swirl higher, higher. She makes a solemn vow: God, if you let this baby live, I will enter the convent. I will become a bride of Christ.

I have lots to think about.

Gertrude, her real name is Gertrude.

Saint Gertrude was a Cistercian nun who entered the convent at the age of five. Cistercians take a vow of silence; they are an enclosed order. At the age of twenty-five, the spouse of her soul revealed Himself to her and favoured her with remarkable visions. She died consumed by love rather than by disease.

I decide I prefer Saint Winifred's story. On the lam from a love-starved suitor. Up and down the steep hills of Wales, she would have given him a run for his money. It would have been an adventure, before the capture, the beheading.

And that tale about being up a gum tree during the Kempsey floods. Surely she would have said, If you let *me* live, I will enter. She would have known that a baby, baptised and innocent, can shoot right into heaven, no questions asked. Why even bargain about a baby? If for some reason it hadn't already been baptised, she could have scooped up some floodwater and done it herself, right there.

But Sister Winifred — Gertrude — how was it for her that day up a gum tree, watching the floodwaters rise?

She is wearing a wide, polished cotton skirt and a white blouse. (What colour hair does she have?) Fighting her way out of the car, quickly quickly. Get the baby out of the nice warm crib and hang on, for Christ's sake hang on. The water is fast and cold even though it's February. It smells of mud and putrefaction.

The floodwaters have spread out across the paddocks so that everything is changed, completely changed.

It tells her that the unimaginable does happen. Only days ago, cows moved along their usual paths by the river, and it seemed as if things would stay like that forever, that that was the problem.

Too late to think about it now. Forget the tracks by the river, forget the slow movement of cows. All that exists today is water, and terrified stock, bellowing in fear, being carried along. Dead stock, dead chooks, miserable still-alive chooks, lounge chairs, sheets of corrugated iron, kero tins, tractor parts, nighties, meat-safes, mattresses, dead wallabies, baling wire. Towards evening, something dark and wet and solid goes by. It could be a pile of blankets; it could be a human corpse.

It could be a time for rash promises.

What kind of God would hold you to a deal made up a gum tree, in extremis?

Sister Winifred advises us to learn some of the poetry off by heart, so we will be able to quote it in the exam.

I learn the passages about the falcon: how he rebuffed the big wind. There are falcons at home; I have seen their swift flickering. I know how they soar on flat wings.

Rita O'Toole learns that poem about a nun taking the veil: I have asked to be where no storms come.

Maria Dwyer doesn't remember to learn anything.

Maybe Rita O'Toole just made up that bit about the baby. Maybe Rita O'Toole's sister, Sister Ambrose, made it up. Maybe Sister Winifred herself made the whole thing up. Maybe postulants pass their limited leisure time telling each other tall stories.

"What sort of falcon is the windhover, exactly?" I demand.

Sister Winifred looks worried. "I'm not sure," she replies. "I think he might have invented it. Because of the way the falcon hovers in the wind. It is an image of Christ, he was referring to Christ," she adds, on firmer ground.

But Hopkins must have known about falcons, mustn't he? She's supposed to be the teacher.

"He said it was the best thing he ever wrote," Sister Winifred says.

She is reaching out to me, in conciliation.

I do not manage to smile.

"They sent him to Ireland," Sister Winifred says. "To teach. He felt cut off from his friends and the countryside that inspired his poetry. 'I am in Ireland now,' he wrote. 'I am at a third remove.'

"This was when he produced his terrible, desolate sonnets," she continues. "He talks about how he has had to 'hoard unheard.'"

Sister Winifred cannot leave this alone.

"In his whole life," Sister Winifred says, "only six people knew he even wrote poetry."

Maria Dwyer is picking her nose.

"He felt his poems were cries like dead letters to someone you love."

I don't know what to say.

"When he was in Ireland," Sister Winifred goes on, "he went to a gathering at a house in Dublin and Yeats was there. The two had nothing to say to one another."

She looks to me.

"Imagine," Sister Winifred says, "the two greatest poets in the same room together and they said nothing. They did not exchange a single word."

I wish this were for Maria Dwyer and Rita O'Toole as well as for me.

It is only two weeks until the end of second term and I get sick. I lie in my bed in the dormitory surrounded by books. I must keep studying. Next term I sit for the exams that will take me to university, where there will be people I can talk to.

Sister Winifred visits.

Our school has been doing better in the Leaving Certificate ever since Sister Winifred arrived. And I am their best bet this year; I am going to show them that convent school girls can do just as well as those brainy kids from the state schools.

"Study, study," Sister Winifred says. "*Ora et labore.*"

"Don't study too hard," she adds.

She is jumpy, uneasy with me.

I lie back and shut my eyes. She goes away.

As soon as she's gone I open my eyes. I feel I've made a mess of something.

I am neither praying nor working, but thinking about Sister Winifred. Not as Sister Winifred, but as Gertrude. (I wish she had a decent real name.)

I should be coming down with her out of the hills, after we'd spent the morning watching the birds.

Her hair would be windblown. She would be leaping from boulder to boulder.

I would have shown her the small falcons.

She would have said, "Ah! bright wings."

One of the old nuns dies. This is the motherhouse for the order in Australia. The old nuns come back here at the end of their lives. You see them sitting on the balcony in the cloister.

Sister Winifred says: "The earthly circle is closing but the heavenly circle is widening."

There is a special requiem mass midmorning. The bishop is coming. Everyone goes, except for the lay sisters, who are working in the dining room, getting the midday meal.

They're all in the chapel, watching the heavenly circle widening.

I am in the dormitory and there is nobody around.

I get up, put on my slippers and dressing gown, and go down the corridor. Past the pictures of the Old Girls. The most famous Old Girls of all—a novelist who writes about people who commit adultery; a Communist—aren't there.

Down the corridor and to the left and you come to the cloister. It is consecrated ground; only nuns are allowed to go there. Except for the priest. If a nun is sick, a priest carrying the host in the ciborium goes into the cloister. A nun hurries ahead of him, ringing a bell.

It is a mortal sin for anyone else to go into the cloister.

But nobody is around. I put one foot, two feet, over the line, and then I am speeding down the corridor. Around the corner, I know, there's a row of three cells. Sister Winifred's is the one with the window facing the tennis court. (Rita O'Toole's intelligence.)

I pass one cell, then another, and here, with the door open, is hers. It must be. Yes, there's the window.

There is a bed. It's made, of course. There's an indentation where her body lies.

A table, not a real desk. She corrects papers late at night, prepares lessons. Here she opens my exercise book, sees my handwriting, reads what I have written.

A kneeler, with one prayer book on it, open at the Litany of the Saints.

No drawers. Where does she keep her underwear? Perhaps they have some communal cupboard down the hall. Her Moddess. Because she must.

But on a peg behind the door, there's a long white flannel nightgown. I hold it in my hands. I bring it up to my cheek.

I lie down in the indentation on the bed and look up at the ceiling. The bed is harder than the ones in the dormitory. Which aren't anything to write home about.

I have to leave a message for her, a sign that I've been here. She has to know.

I get up and look around for a pen. Nothing. Her pen would be in the pocket of her habit, up under her guimpe. I've seen the pen-holder when I've looked at her neck.

Back I go, down the hall, retracing my steps, down the stairs, to the right, out of the cloister. To the dormitory, for a pen.

Then I run back, along the corridor, into the cloister, all the way to her cell. Feeling a bit faint.

I look at the litany of saints. *Sancta Maria Magdalena, Ora pro nobis. Sancta Agnes, Ora pro nobis. Sancta Caecilia, Ora pro nobis. Sancta Agatha, Ora pro nobis. Sancta Anastasia, Ora pro nobis.*

I write in the margins of the litany the one word of Welsh I have memorized from the introduction to the Hopkins poetry book: *cywydd.*

I believe that it means a poem. I don't know how this word might sound in someone's mouth. I do not attempt to pronounce it. I see the letters silently, in my mind.

After I have written this undeniable message in her prayer book, I lie down again.

I stare up at the ceiling and cross my hands over my chest, as if preparing to die.

I think about the falcons at home, hovering, tail feathers fanned.

I think about the wedgies, hunting wallabies, rabbits. Making do with a dead sheep instead, ripping it apart.

Wedge-tailed eagles, eight-foot wing span. Lounging in the thermals, then swooping in a long, lanky sideways dive after prey.

Has Sister Winifred ever seen them mating, in May? One of them coming down upon the other, then pulling out at the last moment, wings half closed.

The lower bird turning on its back in midair, showing its talons.

The pair of them soaring high on upswept wings, sailing out across their countryside, looping and turning in the big wind as they shriek their intentions to the whole wide sky.

That is what I would show her, if she came home with me in the holidays.

I would lead her across the dry yellow grass and up into the hills, among the granite boulders. Get her to look up at the winter shafts of air, the birds. Show her—make her realize—that it was a matter of life and death.

But she will never go anywhere outside the convent. She has chosen. She has been chosen.

Father Kenny

O N a Friday morning in November, as I wrote the last exam of the year at university, my father, fifty miles away, drove the ute out on to the highway and was sideswiped by a semi-trailer. He spent most of the summer months in the local hospital, where he was visited regularly by the new parish priest, Father Kenny McCready. It was across my father's bed that I met Kenny, at the beginning of the long vac.

Or rather, met him again.

Father Kenny was no stranger to our family. He and my brother, Anthony, had been at Springwood and Manly together. Boys of the same diocese, they were ordained in St. Mary's Cathedral. At the time of their ordination—a windy spring day—I was in fourth year at the Angeline Convent and the school choir was on hand to sing the mass. Anthony and the other ordinands prostrated themselves full-length before the altar. They were wearing those long white things they call albs. They were said to be priests forever, in the order of Melchizedek.

The families were out in force. My father was there, and my Aunt Dorothy. That was it for the Careys.

But the McCreadys! Piles of them. They filled up their appointed rows. They overflowed.

The new priests bless the members of their families. It is a damp-eyed moment, a tremendous reversal of power. We Careys were up and blessed and back in our seats, but the Mc-Creadys kept coming. Two of the McCready clan were the Sullivan brothers, who played Rugby League for New South Wales. We had seen their pictures in the paper.

The Kenny McCready who faced me across my father's bed had been a priest for four years. Like his cousins, he was a good footballer. The Young Catholic Workers approved. The older women of the parish approved of him too, as such women do approve of men who are beginning to fill out, men who are young enough to be their sons and who are now striding confidently along in the world.

"Everyone loves young Father McCready," my Aunt Dorothy reported. She was using the word "loves" in a general sense. Also, perhaps, the word "young."

That summer Kenny was thirty-two years old.

I am sitting by my father's bed. My father, at this stage of his illness, cannot speak. He is on oxygen. But he can hear. The nurses show me how to converse.

"MR. CAREY! HOW ARE YER GOING? ALL RIGHT? LOOK-ING GOOD TODAY!"

My father can press hands quite coherently and can, in fact, hear without being shouted at.

"Hello, Dad." A hard press. "I'm putting the calves up and milking Jess." Press. "The chooks are all right." Press. So it goes, the two days a week I spend at the hospital.

John Peters, our neighbour who is taking care of the property, drives to town on Tuesdays and Thursdays. The ute was a write-off in the accident. I could take my bicycle but it's fifteen miles, half of it gravel.

After I pick up some groceries I go to the hospital for the rest of the day. My father and I listen to the test cricket on the radio. I read him the scores from the *Herald*. I read him the trivia from "Column 8." I read him the local news from the *Northern Daily Leader*.

The priest drives me home.

With him, I discuss my courses at uni (Old and Middle English, Latin, Philosophy); Anthony's successes (studying in Rome, he is); the property (John Peters is fixing the fence by the creek, John Peters is going to sow down the pasture). The cricket. The drought. The Kennedy assassination.

On the day of their ordination, they had their pictures taken, all the new priests, standing together in the cathedral grounds. When I look for that picture among my father's things, I find it without any trouble. There is Anthony and there, standing next to Trevor Millane, is Kenny McCready. They look dazed, dazzled. They would have just come off the long retreat that preceded ordination. It was their day, at last. It had happened. *Father* Anthony. My father had blinked and said, "If only your mother. . ."

Of course I know that nothing can happen between me and Kenny McCready. First, there is the obvious. Secondly—a distant second—I am supposed to be going with someone else, a man called Malcolm Travers.

Malcolm Travers was a graduate student in chemistry but he liked to hang around the English department and take part in the play readings it put on. Travers was a good reader and could make people laugh. I remember him in *Waiting for Godot*, chucking turnips around. And in a play by Christopher Fry, getting a good response to the line, "Always fornicate between clean sheets."

Travers was a married man.

I should have been mixing with those boring Newman Society types. But I wasn't.

My time with Travers was spent in his Austin, parked on one of the back roads behind the uni. Travers had an English wife and an infant kid. The wife was unhappy about her new country and disorganized about the kid. Nappies everywhere, Travers said. Kid yowling. Wife in tears. Liquid pouring from every orifice, he added, warming to his theme. Tears, milk, blood, shit.

Disapproving of any newcomer who whinged about Australia (poms, especially) I pressed myself against him, to make up for it. The windows of the Austin fogged up.

I thought that he wouldn't be willing to put up with me for long, being a married man. Yet to my puzzlement he persisted.

When I met Kenny my preoccupation with Travers flew out the window, leaving behind nothing stronger than surprise. How could I be capable of such fickleness? I did not have the kind of face I believed one would need for such a thing. My face is long; I thought of myself as looking like a horse.

I studied that face in the mirror. *O fals Cresseid.* It was not Chaucer's but Henryson's Cresseid I had in mind. She comes to a bad end, that one, *sonkin into cair.*

Kenny has slowed down for the cattle grid. He takes his hand off the gearshift and places it on my right thigh. We bump across the grid. He puts his hand back on the steering wheel. The car moves on.

All summer long I am alone in the house. My father is in hospital. Anthony is at the Gregorium in Rome. My mother is dead. Aunt Dorothy drives out from town regularly, to see how I'm getting along; she always comes on Sunday afternoons. Peters is often on the property, but he rides over the back way, from his own land, and is rarely at the house.

Behind the box gums by the woodheap my father's dogs slouch about (men out of work). At the sound of Kenny's car they bark and pull on their chains in wild distraction. Later, when he goes, their barks diminish only after the last beams of the headlights have swept away in the darkness.

So nobody comes: we have the place to ourselves.

I feed Kenny baked custard and stewed fruit, Big Sister fruitcake. He plays the 78s my mother had bought when we got the electricity hooked up. He opens the piano, plays a few notes, groans, and settles in to play some more. Since my mother's death when I was thirteen, nobody has played the piano much; none of us has the talent for it.

Kenny can play by ear, a fact I find marvellous, extraordinary.

The early hours of the evening are a busy time. People are in their homes with their children. They are listening to the radio. (Some even have TV.) They are dumping the tea leaves in the back garden. If there are no functions at which he is expected, nobody misses the parish priest.

He never leaves later than eight-thirty or a quarter to nine.

Drives back into town, back to the presbytery. And no one knows.

Or so I think.

Kenny had clear and definite plans about how we should be together, what we should do. I concluded that men were like that. Later, when I had other men as lovers, I found myself waiting for them to orchestrate particular, formal gestures, and was confused to find them random, casually opportunistic. It took me some time to put my finger on the possible difference: when it came to planning, Kenny had had at least twenty years.

He took the eiderdown off my father's bed and laid it down in the orchard, beneath the greengage plums, among the sheep droppings.

I want to look at you, he said.

And afterwards, to look with me, up through the leaves to the sky, where the stars were coming out.

He danced with me to my mother's records. His chest was bare and I was wearing my best skirt. He held me solemnly.

These stagey activities unnerved me. We are in the orchard scene, I thought. We are in the dancing scene.

I fortified myself with port, a sophistication recently acquired at uni.

Kenny got the atlas out and showed me how we would drive over to Broken Hill, then down to Adelaide, across to Perth, and up to Geraldton. Imagine, he said. The Indian Ocean.

Together we looked at the map. The impossibly distant, *Indian* Ocean.

A child of the fifties, I came to lovemaking with the expectation that it would be apocalyptic. It had been surrounded with such dense, promising secrecy.

I looked at Kenny's body. I looked and I touched and I felt, and there were many small ridges and hollows.

This is what religion is about, I decided. *This* is his body.

The way in which the items on the mantelshelf could grow dim and fade away seemed to me a powerful revelation. There is the toby jug, a wedding present to my parents. There is the picture of my mother holding Anthony as an infant. She is standing sideways, my mother, holding Anthony with one arm, and bracing herself on the verandah railing with the other. Anthony's shawl hangs in a luxuriant sweep and my mother looks down, devoted. In another photo I am three years old, on the beach at Coogee. Further along the mantelshelf there is a cheap little china giraffe, which I bought years ago as a Mother's Day gift. All of these items move into a static clarity. Finally — and I watch this happening, I wait for it — they recede. They are wiped out.

Afterwards, the plates clack against each other as I take them down from the cupboard. The knife, sliding through the fruit-cake, is met with a satisfying resistance. The cake slides onto the white plate and sits there, magnificently solid, a central dark rectangle.

I develop a name for it. Quotidian happiness. I look the adjective up in the dictionary, to make sure it's what I want. It's what I want all right. If Kenny and I . . . we could have quotidian happiness. I believe I already do have it with him. Even the gate to the orchard closes with its own, excellent creak.

One evening Kenny sat down at the piano and played and sang. I recognized the song from St. Patrick's Day concerts: "Down by the Salley Gardens." "She bid me take life easy," Kenny sang, "as the grass grows on the weirs; But I was young and foolish, and now am full of tears."

I knew I would have to pay.

I am sitting by my father's bed and Kenny has not come.

My father is not making the recovery that has been expected and there is talk of sending him down to the Royal Prince Alfred, to see what can be done. I cannot hear Kenny's foot-steps in the hall and he does not stand there, filling the door-way. Instead, the nurse has come to announce that visiting hours are over. I am being thrown out. I have to get up and walk over to the door, down the corridor, down the steps and out into the street.

I must set my face in place. The jaw. Think about keeping the jaw sitting quietly beneath the teeth. Breathe. Remember to breathe.

In the Middle English I had studied, lovers fell *doun in swoun.* I had laughed. I had not known, then, that they were describing a physical fact.

Walk along; I am walking along. I am walking home alone because he did not come. I will have to walk all the way home. Fifteen miles.

Listen to the cicadas, singing. Singing of dust and summer and seven years in the ground. At St. Angela's the chapel smelled of cool stone and candles; then the incense. *Adoremus in aeternum,* we sang. I shall love you for ever and ever. Outside, the cicadas sang that soon we would be breaking up for the summer holidays. We wouldn't have to get up at six o'clock every morning. We could eat all the biscuits and lollies we wanted. We were going home.

Here is John Peters and he is asking me if I want a lift. John Peters, innocuous as his name, does not ask questions. Does not say, How come the priest isn't driving you home? How come the priest—that priest of yours—didn't show up today? John Peters is a silent, rural man and thank God for that. John Peters, held up today at the ram sales, is that mildest kind of believer, a four-wheeler Anglican (baptisms, weddings and funerals). Wouldn't know what all the fuss was about.

How would it be to be John Peters? What would it be like not to have to worry?

I put my arm on the window: casual, normal. Tell him about the Royal Prince Alfred; any day now. My father. Not what they expected.

In the gorges to the east there were bushfires. The sun went over in a haze and Kenny did not come. In the orchard the apricots ripened and fell. The lorikeets carried on like a bunch of drunks. After a week I took a bath. I washed my hair. I ate.

I lit the copper and took down the curtains and washed them. They had not been washed since my mother's death and some of them fell apart in my hands. I fished out the survivors. I rinsed, dried, starched and ironed them. Those I could not wash I hung on the clothesline and poked at with a broom.

I put the blankets in the bathtub and jumped up and down on them. I cleaned the silver. When I went to town with John Peters I bought varnish and did the hallway and the lounge room, where the carpets didn't reach. My mother had been a determined woman—witness the way she had kept Anthony's name intact—and she had washed and shone as if it were a language she was fluent in. What a falling off there had been over the seven years! Stains on the tablecloths and, in the cracks between the lino, a steady accretion.

There was a lot to get on with.

My Aunt Dorothy, pleased to see I was keeping busy, said it was high time I left uni for good. The place was packed with Protestants and atheists who refused to wash. I should come home and take care of my father, who needed me. It was what my mother would have wanted, she said. (I think the housework really got her hopes up.)

What my father wanted, I countered, was for her to move out from town to take care of things. After I'd gone back to uni, I added hastily. With my aunt I felt loose and wild and bitter. And, for the first time, powerful.

So Aunt Dorothy, who had put in ten years with her bed-ridden mother (that was the phrase we always used, bed*ridden*), came out to the property to do it all over again for my father. Who in time recovered, and carried on.

Back I went to university.

And no letter came.

I ran into Travers in the student union.

"It's you!" he said, as if he'd been looking for me everywhere. "Where've you been?"

"Haven't got the plague, you know," he said.

No, I thought, it is I who am the leper. But I will not repent.

What have they done with him? What has happened? Have they punished and shamed him?

Does he despise me for what I did? Does he pray for forgiveness? Forgiveness for me?

Well I wasn't sorry. Not in the least.

If only he would write!

Was he really not going to write to me? Not *ever*?

My one satisfaction was that I could tell Travers I had met someone who made fooling around in the Austin fatuous.

But Travers was a changed man. His wife's stitches had healed up. Everything was back in working order, he was happy to report. Up and running smoothly. And the baby. The baby was sitting up and looking around taking everything in, curious little monkey.

"You really should see the baby," he said, rhetorically. "Really, you should."

So. He was not going to ask and I was not going to be able to say no. I was to be denied even this one thing.

I stomped off.

Kenny was waiting to contact me. One day he would show up and I would leave whatever I was doing, leave immediately. I would leave the ink still wet on the page and the coffee warm in its mug. We would drive to Broken Hill, to Adelaide, to Perth, then up to Geraldton, and nobody would bother us, nobody would know where we were, who we were. He could get a job teaching Latin. He might show up in need of clothes. I had one of Anthony's old sweaters. It would do in a pinch. The black trousers wouldn't be too noticeable.

When I came back from lectures, he'd be there in the parking lot, waiting for me. He'd be tapping at my window at three in the morning, sounding like the wind. I would hide him in my room. (He could use a bucket.)

It would be like the French Resistance. I would smuggle him safely out. Home for the May holidays, I went to work on Aunt Dorothy. Turned away from her, arranging groceries in the cupboard, I asked her about the new parish priest.

"Old parish priest, you mean," she said.

Father Mulchay was back, and he was much better now, he was his old self again.

Mulchay hit the grog, everyone knew it.

I was forced to push on.

"What happened to, you know, Father McCready?"

"I couldn't say for sure." Pause. But she had heard something, come to mention it. He'd been transferred to another diocese, was it Grafton or Maitland? Yes, down to the Maitland diocese, that was it.

The following September, she had some more news. A friend of hers had been talking to Father Mulchay—his problem had come back again — and she said that he said that Father McCready had not been well. Not at all well. Bit of a breakdown, in fact.

Where was he?

She didn't know. If I was so keen to find out, Aunt Dorothy said, I could go to mass on Sunday for a change and ask Father Mulchay myself. It was all very well and good over the Christmas holidays when I was out here on my own without a car. I was excused. But now here she was, with the Holden, and there was nothing to stop me from going. What my mother would have said, she didn't know. And hated to think.

They had driven him crazy and locked him up somewhere.

They would do it. This was the mob that brought you strappado.

Why had he let himself be locked up in a loony bin? I knew what went on in places like Callan Park: they put them in the cold showers and beat them with broom handles. It had all come out in the Sunday papers.

Maybe they had a place like that, especially for priests. Did they make him practise mortification of the flesh? In the twentieth century, today, Jesuits still whipped themselves, and a lot of others did, too. They kept this nice and quiet, but they did it, just the same.

It was in this state of mind that I completed my degree. I became one of those drab young women who stand at the edges of things, who can't scrounge up anyone to go out with them, not even to the college ball.

I listened to what the others said about this one and that one: why doesn't he phone, why didn't he tell me, what am I going to say to my parents? When they sat in the common room in tears, needing to be comforted with cups of tea, I felt a sour vindication.

Weekends were the worst. They closed the library at lunchtime on Saturday. Whoever heard of a university library that wasn't open on Sunday?

Because he neither wrote nor came, and for want of anything else to do, I studied and did quite well. Well enough, in fact, to get a scholarship to go overseas, to graduate school.

They asked, "What were you doing when Kennedy was assassinated?" And I did not answer, truthfully, "I was asleep." Instead, I said, "I was falling in love with a priest." When this went down rather splendidly, I amended it to, "I was in bed with a priest." But the success of having had something smart to say turned out to be not what I'd been looking for, after all. It was the particulars I was interested in. Kenny and me. Me and my Kenny McCready.

With my new lover, I was more determined. Did he have any idea what it had meant? The strain? Didn't he *realize*? We were flying in the face of God. No need of mirrors, Kenny and I. We had God the Father, God the Son and God the Holy Ghost getting their almighty knickers in a twist about what was going on.

"Well, move over Copernicus," my young man said. A kind young man, really. Fed up with me. "Give Galileo the news. No, the sun is not a fixed body in the heavens. Lo, it has come to earth and dwells among us, although we know not where. What we do know, my fellow sinners, is that it is shining, shining constantly, out of this Kenny-priest-guy's ass."

It was like that, with me, for a long time.

If it wasn't for my brother, Anthony, I would have lost track of Kenny entirely.

When I came home after years overseas, I went to see Anthony. He was back from Rome and teaching at the Manly seminary.

It seems to me—and this must be a commonplace observation—that the seminary at Manly contrasts sharply with the goings on below. On the hill, the house of celibacy. In the streets, at least three of the seven deadly sins on daily parade —lust, gluttony, sloth.

This was where Kenny had spent the final years of study for the priesthood. Perhaps it was the bouncing Manly sun and the flash of bodies that gave him a sense of the possibilities.

My brother strolled with nonchalance among the hedonists in the streets. He sucked on his disgusting pipe and gave me the news. About my father's funeral, which I hadn't come home for. How John Peters bought the property, stock and all. How the house now stands empty and the orchard is going wild.

After family matters, the conversation moved on to more general topics. Trevor Millane, now a monsignor, is secretary to a bishop. Travels a lot. Kenny McCready. "Do you remember him?" Anthony asked. "Oh yes," I said. "I remember him. Ordained with you, wasn't he?"

Kenny left the priesthood. Went to America, to Los Angeles. Is doing his doctorate in marine biology at UCLA. They'd lost touch, but Trevor got his address through the family, and wrote to him. Kenny wrote back.

All the time I was in the States, Kenny was there, too. I could have dialled L.A. information and got his number. Just like that. I could have gone out to the coast on a Greyhound bus. If only I had known.

I would have done it, too. I would have gone out there and made a fool of myself.

The letters to Trevor continue. Kenny is a good correspondent, after all. (I never would have guessed.) During my annual January visits with Anthony I get the occasional update. Kenny is working on his post-doc. Kenny is moving to Oregon in the northern spring.

The peripatetic Trevor goes off to Oregon on a junket with his bishop. Meets Kenny and his wife.

His wife.

Spends an evening with them. No, no children.

What's his wife like? A very pleasant woman, according to Trevor. Canadian. A biologist, also.

Pleasant: agreeable to the mind, feelings or senses. To all these three, one hopes. And does he have quotidian happiness with her?

I was wrong, of course, about the word quotidian. Quotidian: a sturdy cargo ship is working its way across the Pacific. Night falls and still the solid thing ploughs on, rusted out but enduring, tough.

There is more. Kenny has broken into print. His book, *Nudibranchs of the Northeast Pacific,* is for sale in the local bookstores there. Trevor brought some copies back.

"It seems," said Anthony, mildly, "Kenny has given up on God and taken up with slugs instead."

In his introduction Kenny explains that his speciality is nudibranchs. Pronounced "branks," he tells us.

He thanks "all the brankers up and down the coast."

The nudibranchs are described in taxonomist's detail. But Kenny enthuses, too. "These delicate small animals," he writes, "are known as the butterflies of the sea. They astound and delight, simply because they are."

Anthony and I walked along the Corso. My annual visit, again.

I told him that my marriage—to the kind young man—was going down the toilet. I used the shallow, ugly phrase deliberately, to keep things at a distance.

And despite all my resolutions I began to weep: familiar, tedious, boring tears. "I'm so fed up with being like this," I said, to my brother.

In the middle of the Corso, Anthony embraced me, held me close. As he did this I was aware of the big sandstone seminary on the hill behind me, the seminarians.

I told him that priests had come a long way. He laughed. He knows what I think of the Church.

"Since when?" he asked. "Since when have we come a long way?"

We went for ice creams in the blue and white place with all the clocks. Midnight in New York. That means 9:00 P.M. on the West Coast.

A night of early dark in the middle of winter: Kenny is inside. In his room there are hardwood floors, bookshelves with glass doors, Persian rugs. Kenny is listening to a violin concerto. Bruch, he is listening to the Bruch. He's seated by the fire, which right at this moment flares up with a bright sodium flame.

Outside, where I am, there is the cold smell of dead wet leaves.

I see his pleasant, Canadian wife (a biologist also) come into the room.

Anthony, Trevor and I are sitting at a picnic table on the back verandah of the cottage they now rent each January, for a fortnight's break at the beach. Drinking passable cask wine and picking at the last of the mango and passionfruit salad. Talking about nothing much. The king tides, the cyclonic disturbance off the coast.

I'm up for the weekend.

The sun has set and the mosquitoes are beginning to bite. Anthony has brought out a mosquito coil.

I can smell the frangipani along the side fence — always stronger at night—and the surf.

"These two add up to the most romantic smell on earth," Anthony says.

A decade ago I would have pounced on this at once, demanding to know what romance might smell like in heaven, what priests could claim to know about romance.

Now I don't bother.

We have a few more glasses of wine and Trevor tells us a story about Kenny.

When the three of them were in the seminary together in Springwood, in the Blue Mountains, they couldn't listen to a radio for months on end.

During the Suez Crisis Kenny lay on the floor with his ear to the floorboards, trying to hear the radio the priests were listening to in the room below.

"It was enough to give you piles," Trevor says. "Piles of the earhole."

"It wasn't cold at that time of the year," Anthony says.

"Bullshit, mate. It was freezing all year round in the seminary," Trevor says.

Then Trevor and Anthony go off to play Scrabble in Latin. They do this only when they're at the beach. Each year, they claim, they remember less and less.

Trevor says, "The grey cells are dropping their bundles."

Anthony says, "We pray to remember."

"*De profundis clamavi ad te, Domine,*" Trevor says.

Anthony takes it up: "*Domine, exaudi orationem meam.*"

I can smell the smoke from the mosquito coil, mixing in with the surf and frangipani.

I watch the mosquito coil: the small hot knob where it burns, the white ash as it falls, the way the smoke curls upwards and then vanishes.

Breasts

1

It's Tuesday afternoon and Lex Maguire is perched on the edge of Ruth's desk.

"Peter and I won't speak to one another," Lex tells Ruth.

Lex will be there with her, incognito. Two strangers in their public servant skirts.

"Why is that?" Ruth asks.

"We have to be so careful," Lex says. "His wife knows all those people."

They're going to stay only until Peter has finished speaking; they won't hang around for the herbal tea afterwards.

"Peter says he doesn't know if he'd be able to pull it off, having me there," Lex explains. "With everybody milling about socializing."

"What does he think he might do?" Ruth asks.

Lex and Peter rolling round the meeting floor together. Lex's soft blouse and then Lex's breasts, white and surprising.

2

Lex and Peter take separate trains to a distant suburb, to rendezvous in a shopping mall. They sit in a coffee shop and hold hands. They anguish.

"At this rate," Ruth says, "you'll be able to keep it up for years."

At the Easter weekend, in two days' time, Lex and Peter are going up the Central Coast together. They are booked into a hotel room with an ocean view.

"We're leaving on Thursday around noon," Lex says.

Maundy Thursday, Ruth thinks. Christ washed the feet of the apostles to prove that he was just an ordinary bloke like them. Nothing human is alien to me, He said, looking around for a towel.

Lex, on Ruth's desk, goes over the plans.

There is Lex's husband. There are Lex's two children, boys, aged seven and ten. There is Peter's wife. All of these, to be deceived.

3

At lunchtime Lex goes swimming.

"I walked into the shower with all my clothes on," Lex says, laughing. "I forget things," she says. "I forget everything these days."

"I don't have that problem myself," Ruth says.

After work Lex and Ruth go shopping for Lex's new underwear. A bra that does up, and — more to the point — can be undone, at the front.

"Four whole nights together," says Lex, her voice full of the danger, the luxury.

"You two will really be able to talk," Ruth says.

Lex giggles.

"Watch late night television," Ruth says.

"Listen to big band music," Ruth goes on.

4

Ruth and Lex walk down from Newtown station, along King Street, past dark empty storefronts and a few trendy antique stores. Gentrification has just begun to put out tendrils into this inner-city Sydney suburb, where the night still belongs to the hoons. Who are driving up and down.

When they get a glance of Lex's slender body, short skirt and long, fair hair, they shout abuse.

"Dick features!" Lex shouts after them.

Neither Ruth nor Lex has been here before. They search for the street number, and find it, a dusty hall, where people gather to discuss threats to life on earth, what must be done before it is too late. (Perhaps it is already too late.)

5

Out of the shadows, he comes, Peter. Sits down at the table. Sideways glance at Lex. Quick, nervy toss of the head. There's a blood vessel in his forehead, throbbing. The light shines on his face and one can see he's just shaved.

He's younger than Lex, who is years younger than Ruth.

But nonetheless embroiled: wife, home, mortgage.

What does his wife surmise?

Wives don't surmise; they know.

6

Peter's getting ready to start. He steals a look at Lex.

He has a little pile of books in front of him on the desk, to one side. Later, he'll be reading quotes out of them.

He does have a nice, trim little body, Ruth notes.

Ruth thinks, in an unsentimental, uncharged way, that it's been a long time since she last stepped into a dusty meeting room like this one, a long time since her lovemaking was fuelled by the desire to make a difference, to put things right.

It is pleasant to be sitting here, beside Lex. To be finally getting a look at thou art Peter (and I will give to thee the keys of the kingdom of heaven).

"He's very cute," Ruth whispers to Lex.

Encouraged, Lex whispers back, "He's *gorgeous.*"

"He'd look great with his shirt off. Like Sting," Ruth murmured into Lex's ear. Mixing memory and desire.

Lex's face fills with pleasure.

7

Twenty-five years ago, on the other side of the world, in Vancouver: David, telling her about multiplying the revolution; Ruth, with her mouth open.

It's all still there, inside. Rolling around like wash in a dryer. Like cells in the body.

8

Ruth is standing outside the hotel (continuous entertainment). She is looking at the bookstore across the street.

The sun is shining, tentatively. It is the kind of winter's day that warns us not to expect too much, to be glad for the grace we have.

Ruth can see David inside the store, when he passes in front of the window.

See his long black hair.

David, the new father, who says that this must stop, that now he has responsibilities, that they cannot go on as before.

Any minute now, she's going to cross the street. She'll go into the bookstore and sit in her usual spot behind the door, beneath the poster of Che.

Ruth reaches into her purse and takes out a cigarette.

9

"What will it be like?" Ruth asked.

This was in the early days, right at the beginning.

"The state," said David, "will have withered away."

Ruth imagined a courtyard on a sunny afternoon: vines are hanging from trellises and the almond trees are in blossom. The gate to the courtyard is open, and beyond is a broad street — no cars, just people and dogs and bicycles. It's like heaven, rather boring. Except that over there, on a wooden bench beneath the almond blossoms, Simone de Beauvoir is eating peach ice cream and having opinions about it.

"Complete personal autonomy," David said. "No relationships based on ownership."

He was looking at her breasts when he said this.

"We are more free because we are fulfilled," David said. "And are more fulfilled because we are free."

Then he slipped his hand under her sweater. Discreetly, because they were in the bookstore.

Bravely, he looked her in the eyes.

10

Ruth's husband is doing his post doc in chemistry, that's why they are in Vancouver.

Ruth learns how to make meat lasagna with green salad and garlic bread, cheesecake for dessert. She goes on Dr. Atkins's high-protein diet. She enrolls in Spanish classes. She reads *The Second Sex.* She makes friends among the women.

The women sit in one another's kitchens, during the day-time. They talk about babies, then, in quieter, more careful voices, about husbands. Their demands.

We both want it, Ruth says. There is no conceivable reason, Ruth says — joking, to make light of things — why it hasn't happened yet.

But when she thinks about becoming pregnant by her husband, Ruth imagines a bull terrier, its teeth sunk into the bull's neck. The dog is hanging on and hanging on, although the blood pours down its small body and its feet are right off the ground.

She's not sure who is who.

11

The first time Ruth saw David's wife, her stomach careened downward, like a lift, an elevator, out of control in the movies. (A second later, you will hear the villain scream.)

Things have gone beyond the stage of sulking about husbands and wives, David said.

He gave her a book about private property and the family.

David's wife was five, six months pregnant.

12

David showed her pictures of Che and she saw right away that the posterized Che, beard and beret, did not do him justice. His face was rounder, more open; he could look ironic, humble, tired. Ernesto, the worrier, the doctor. Who puffed happily

on a cigar, and almost choked with asthma. Of Irish and Spanish descent: Argentinian, Cuban, internationalist. Couldn't
hold a tune. Allergic to fish.

Che met Fidel on one of those cold nights in Mexico, and
right away they were friends for life. The *Granma* was due to
sail, and Che was in jail, an illegal alien. He urged Fidel to
keep to his plan, to go on without him.

But Fidel waited.

"I will not abandon you," said Fidel to Che. *No te
abandonaré.*

Che had deep crinkly smile lines that went out from his
eyes. The clear eyes of the believer.

When he took his beret off, his hair was like a furry animal,
the kind you want to sink your face into.

David said, "Your political education is coming along
nicely."

He kissed the back of her neck.

13

David's wife didn't come to meetings regularly, only once in a
while.

Ruth was supposedly out with some of the girls she met at
Spanish class. Her husband said he was glad she was making
new friends.

After the meeting they cleared away the chairs and danced.

David's wife gave her the dutiful, vague smile of one who
knows that newcomers must be made to feel welcome, it's good
politics.

Ruth was wearing a pale blue angora sweater. She thought
of it as her bunny sweater.

At the edge of the room, David watched.

At last he came over to dance with her. His hands reached
out, as if casually.

"You love the way your nipples stand up and people can see
them," David whispered. "Don't you."

"People?" she challenged.

14

What they were doing (of course) was smashing monogamy.

They were going to have a wedding cake with "Smash Monogamy" written on the top.

First dance, David promised, would be with his ex. After the one with you, he amended.

They lay in the back room of the bookstore, on a makeshift bed of a Mexican blanket thrown over books from the left presses. After they had made love, sometimes David mock-fucked her, pushing against her, saying: smash mon-nog-arrggh-ME.

A stack of *Wages, Price and Profit* poked at her kidneys.

I must read more of this stuff, she thought. I really must try to keep up.

She laughed, pushing back, saying: smash, smash smash.

15

They walked down to the water, Ruth and David. She sat on a log and looked out at the wet black of the inlet and the solid black of Hollyburn Mountain, the mountain that stands behind Vancouver like an immovable backdrop.

Across the water, in Lions Gate Hospital, David's wife was waiting for her baby. Lying in wait.

David slid both his hands onto Ruth's breasts, sneakily, coming up on her from behind.

"Ah," he said, feeling her and looking up at the sky. "So fine."

It seems to Ruth, looking back, that she must have then thought of David's wife's breasts, daily growing bigger and bigger, audacious with their purpose.

There were huge ships at anchor in the middle of the inlet. Their lights shivered in the water.

"Think of the guys out there," Ruth said.

"Playing cards, jerking off," David said.

"No," Ruth said. "Waiting for something to happen."

16

In one of the graduate student huts on UBC campus, Ruth cooked her husband's evening meal (pork chops, mushroom soup for gravy).

Her husband reached up in the doorway, put his arms on the door jamb, talked on and on about his day at the lab.

The lab: such a convenient, generic term.

The temple will be rent asunder, Ruth thought, and immediately felt better. She imagined the rows of huts torn apart, open to the weather, uninhabitable.

Kitchenware, bedding, books, clothes, records, all mixed in with mud, gravel. Her husband, coming home very late from the lab, will survey the debris and won't even be able to make out where their place had been.

Ruth poked at the chops.

Something was going to happen that would change everything. She knew it, she just knew it.

When it did, she would be released from her place by this stove, this man.

17

David and Ruth went hiking up Hollyburn Mountain. They lay down in the tender spring grass and took off each other's shirts. To torment him, she rubbed her breasts lightly across David's chest. In happy co-operation, he groaned.

When Che came down out of the Sierra Maestra, David said, there were 160 guerrillas and 10,000 of Batista's men. Then Che was in Santa Clara and all around him campesinos, everyone exhausted, dirty, and just grinning from ear to ear.

But in Bolivia, in the dense scrub by the Ñancahuazú River, the going was slow. Ernesto would not leave his wounded.

Ruth unpacked the picnic while David rolled another joint. She considered her chances, with David.

18

Ruth holds the cigarette in her young, smooth hand. In a minute or two, any minute now, she is going to cross the street and go into the bookstore. She will sit in her once familiar spot, behind the door.

David will say, What did you expect? Did you really expect it could go on and on, forever?

She will hear those words and she will not be able to understand them.

Later, she will think: But I did expect it. I did. Something marvellous and new had been about to happen. It had been inevitable.

The smoke will curl upwards, slow in the heated air, curl up to the poster of Che, right up to the tip of the red star on his beret.

Che is already dead. Laid out on that laundry tub in Bolivia.

19

Peter has been working his way through the issue: what is really happening, the local loss, the public loss. Ruth can tell by the change in his voice that now he is beginning the most important part of his talk: what does the future hold?

Ruth spent this morning at the Sarah Fisher Hospital for women, in Redfern. Sarah Fisher is a stern, egalitarian place: lots of waiting on dull chairs, a smell of sweat, and a fine view of the surrounding Sydney slums.

The great advantage of the Sarah Fisher Hospital is that after the waiting and the interview with the nurse and the waiting and the mammogram and the waiting, there is finally the interview with the doctor. By the end of your stint there you have the news, and the doctor's note in your big bag to prove it.

You undress to the waist and they take your breast and put it on a plate.

This will feel quite firm, the nurse says.

20

In the next cubicle at the Sarah Fisher Hospital, a woman is speaking in a language Ruth does not understand. Someone (a nurse?) is acting as translator.

"We will need to get in touch with a family member right away," the doctor says. "Ask her who she has."

"Just a little lump," the woman says. "A touch of mastitis." She says this one word very carefully, in English.

Mastitis?

"Tell her it's more serious than that," the doctor says. "Does she understand?" he asks.

"Just a little lump," the woman says. You can tell from her tone that she remains bright and undeterred.

"Tell her," the doctor says — and his voice grows dignified and gentle — "tell her we will do the very best we can."

"A touch of mastitis," the woman insists.

"Does she understand?" the doctor asks again.

21

Ruth sits in her cubicle, waiting for the doctor to get to her.

She is reading an article about the arctic fox. The arctic fox can detect a mouse moving under two feet of ice.

22

After Ruth left the hospital she missed the train at Redfern. She sat on the platform, waiting.

Maybe she was Macedonian, that woman in the next cubicle. The words she had spoken sounded Greek, only not.

Did Macedonian sound like Greek? Or was it a Slavic language?

Ruth crossed one leg, then the other; she held the fabric of her skirt between finger and thumb, pleating and unpleating it. In her mind, she was praying. Not really, she can't really pray, she's not a believer. But she was saying to herself: Please, please, let this turn out to be just another ordinary day; let this be the kind of day you end up forgetting simply because you can't remember them all.

Ruth looked at the geraniums on the far platform nobody uses, where the country trains lumber on through. These geraniums grow in old rubber tires fashioned into the shape of swans.

Somebody is proud of them, and tends them with care.

23

Peter is rustling his papers, and soon he will be finished. Lex reaches for her bag, getting ready to go.

Ruth watches Peter as he sees Lex get up, watches the awareness in his face.

There passes, very quickly, from Peter to Lex, a message of breathtaking anxiety.

So it is mutual, Ruth thinks. Requited. He's right into it too.

He shouldn't be worrying so much, what's the point?

Heaps of time for that later.

Peter swallows. His hand reaches out for the glass of water.

24

They take the train home to Ruth's place.

Lex sits in Ruth's kitchen, looking around at the stove, the coffee mugs, the chopping board, for reassurance.

Under the irrational rules of deception, Ruth realizes, it helps Lex to have been here, even briefly.

Here they have allegedly been all evening, working late.

So Lex did come here, sometime after work. That much is true.

Ruth drives Lex home to the suburbs, down Victoria Road, past the frenetic car lots, up over Gladesville Bridge—with the window down for some sweet cold air from the river—over the hills and on into a pleasant street, to park in front of a small brick house with an orange-tiled roof.

"Well," says Lex, wanting to talk about Peter, not wanting to get out of the car and go into that other life. Not just yet.

Because there is a light shining in the front bedroom.

"Seriously," says Lex. "What did you think of him?"

Because inside, awake, is her husband. Who is a kind, honest, irreproachable man.

25

It's a clear autumn night and out here, in the suburbs, the stars are out.

"Look at that, the Milky Way," Ruth says.

They each stick a head out a car window and look up.

"I'll be looking at the stars but I'll be seeing you," Lex sort-of sings.

Ruth pictures Lex's children, asleep in the back bedroom. Her two boys would be in their bunk beds, arms thrown up in sleep, oblivious, as the vulnerable are, of their colossal demands.

On the other side of the car, Lex sighs.

"What are you thinking about, right at this moment?" Ruth asks, deliberately. Lex wants to talk.

Lex turns from the night into the warmth of the car.

Lex's face has a naked quality. It is flooded with that exclusive, exalted, particular dizziness: *in love.*

Ruth can hear the doctor's voice. His tone of restrained concern — for her, just as sincerely as for the woman in the next cubicle. But there was no need. Surely?

They need to take a look, to check things out.

Nothing more.

On Thursday night there will be a bed available for her at Sarah Fisher. Maundy Thursday. Maundy, from the Middle English word, command.

Surprising how quickly they can get their act together when they want to.

There's no reason to make a big deal out of it.

Don't start carrying on. Not right now. Not yet.

Probably just a huge fuss over nothing.

Everything will work out all right. Bound to.

Best not to even think about it.

Think about Lex.

Lex's breasts, warm and gentle, sleeping under her sweater. But with Peter, this Easter weekend, up the Central Coast, in the hotel room with the ocean view—their nipples deeply coloured, fierce with sex. She can see why Peter . . .

"Two more nights till we go," Lex says, and her breath becomes thick as she says this. "Two more nights."

Uncle Reg and the Wide Brown Land

UNCLE Reg's been in a fight. He can't use his hand, so he's pushing in the clutch and Annie's operating the gearshift. She grabs it with both hands.

It's chilly in the truck. Out to the right, beyond the dunes, is the Southern ocean, with an Antarctic wind blowing. To the left, salt flats stretch away in the dark, up into the desert. (Here and there some fool has put up a fence and presumed to call this land his own.)

As the Dodge lurches along the road, Uncle Reg is reciting:
"Murder, bloody murder
—third, mate, get her into third—
yelled the man from Ironbark."
Annie is twelve years old, home from boarding school.
She is happy.

Uncle Reg goes into town and gets into a stoush (his word). Then he stumbles around to Aunty Marie's to get cleaned up. Annie's been waiting round there for ages.

"What on earth have you been up to, you big bad boy," Aunty Marie says, bringing warm water and Dettol.

Uncle Reg laughs, affirmed. He leans his head against Aunty Marie's stomach.

"For crying out loud," says Aunty Marie. She smiles at Annie over his head. Drawing her in.

Annie is proud of Uncle Reg.

Uncle Reg can take on anyone.

They aren't related, Aunty Marie and Uncle Reg. Annie just calls her Aunty. But Uncle Reg is her real uncle. He is her father's brother.

Aunty Marie is the town bike. Annie doesn't know what that means; not really; not yet.

Annie lives with Uncle Reg because of what happened on Christmas Eve, 1950.

Annie's mother and father went for a dip at Noralunga.

Drowned, most likely. Perhaps taken by a great white.

White pointers, everyone called them then.

At first, Annie was sent to live with the old, old aunts: Miss Brown and Miss Muriel Brown.

Annie's the centre of the room, although they're pretending she's not. It's polite to think one thing but look like you're thinking another. They're sitting in the lounge room, drinking tea and eating cakes from the traymobile. Annie watches their necks as they swallow.

What they really want to do is stare. Five years old: her parents carried away by the Southern ocean.

They take quick, darting looks.

One woman — her mouth is full of teeth — offers Annie a piece of caraway seed cake. Annie accepts. She even smiles. Everyone is pink and gratified. Annie can feel her smile, launched into the room, feel the ripples it is making. They are all taking the credit for it, but humbly, as they should.

Annie tries it once more. Again, it works. There is a murmur in the room, soft and warm and willing.

This is how it is going to be, from now on.

Then things fall apart: they all get up and they leave her, except for the two old, old aunts.

Annie crawls behind the sofa. They fish her out.

Who do they think they are?

Miss Brown and Miss Muriel Brown are the sisters of Annie's mother. Mild, timid women, the Misses share their lives with two stern young men on the piano. One was killed at Gallipoli and the other, in France, only days (hours, minutes) before the Armistice.

On Sunday there is the joint to prod, there are baked potatoes, baked pumpkin, then bread and butter pudding before a lie down. No wonder that the Misses are constructed out of slabs. A slab at the top front, like a concrete shelf.

In evenings they sit on either side of the fire, vying.

"Have the rug, Muriel, you know how you have to take care of yourself." (You are weak and I am strong.)

"No thank you, dear. I'm up and down all the time." (I do all the work around here, unlike some people.)

The Misses keep jars of lollies in their rooms: humbugs and bull's-eyes. Annie knows that when she is asleep, they get their jars out and gobble, selfishly, without sharing.

The Misses don't know how to draw the face on the boiled egg. They don't know that Annie must always have the brownest one, the darkest. They don't know how to cut soldiers to dip in.

Annie throws the egg, cup and all, on to the lino. It smashes.

The Misses gasp.

Annie wets the bed. Miss Muriel takes her into her own. Annie lies adrift in the windy night while Miss Muriel heaves and bobs. Her nightgown is hiked up around her belly. She is all wrinkled like a savoy cabbage. She gives off cabbage farts.

Annie knows she has to run away.

A neighbour finds her in the morning, curled up in the park, asleep in the fragrant detritus of the blue gums.

It is decided. She is to be sent away to the country, to Uncle Reg and Aunty Betty's.

"She needs a man's hand," the Misses say. Ominously.

Uncle Reg puts Annie's suitcase in the boot.

"Hop in, mate," he says.

They are going to Uncle Reg and Aunty Betty's place. Aunty Betty doesn't come with Uncle Reg in the car.

Aunty Betty is expecting.

As Uncle Reg drives away, heading for the Port Road, he says: "Wave to the walruses, mate."

Walruses? Perfect!

It is wash day. They have to wait until the fire beneath the copper has died down. The sheets and clothes are on the clothesline, a great white billowing. Aunty Betty tests the water by putting in her left elbow. When it's right Annie is allowed to get in. She sits down in the deep warm water. Reg takes the stick (bleached from poking the sheets about) and uses it to swirl the water. He moves it carefully around and around the edge of the copper.

Whoaa, he says. Whoaa.

Aunty Betty holds a towel. Aunty Betty has a big stomach. Expecting.

Aunty Betty wears a wide frock with a starched white collar.

Annie is their dress rehearsal.

See how easy it's going to be, how familiar somehow, how it will work, for them.

Uncle Reg picks Annie up, out of the copper, and sits her on the warm bricks, for Aunty Betty to dry.

"Off we go, mate," he says. Naked, on his shoulders, she rides out of the wash house and into the yard. Gallopy gallopy, she shouts. Uncle Reg climbs up on top of the woodheap. There's a silver daytime moon in the sky.

"The moon is up," Reg recites, "the stars are bright; the wind is fresh and free / We're out to seek for gold tonight / across the silver sea."

The lights are on in the middle of the night and there are neighbours, standing there. Staring.

Uncle Reg yells and pushes at them.

Aunty Betty is carried out under a sheet. Nobody's watching Annie, so she goes into the bedroom. She sees the blood.

There is the panicky smell of big trouble.

Aunty Betty does not come home. She goes to heaven instead.

Annie knows they really are in big trouble, her and Uncle Reg.

The front door is made of mottled glass. Uncle Reg kicks it in.

Then Uncle Reg is gone for days. The neighbours make Annie sleep at their place.

She cries out in her sleep.

But Uncle Reg comes for her and together they leave the house and move out to the shack. It's made out of corrugated iron held together by fencing wire. It sings in the wind.

From this shack, Uncle Reg goes fishing. Mulloway are the best. These he takes into Goolwa; from there they go to the fish shop in Adelaide where Miss Muriel buys them on Friday morning, calling them butterfish.

The shack is perched among the limestone outcrops by the lagoon. It's pretty ordinary. It has fibro walls and real windows. Along one wall there's a wood stove with an open fire beside it. The table is covered with oilcloth, and Reg has two chairs to sit at table in, and two lounge chairs by the fire. At one end of the shack, Reg has rigged up an alcove with a curtain down its middle: the bedrooms. For storage, he's nailed some butter-boxes together. You hang your clothes on nails on the wall.

Fish, rope, bacon, wood smoke, tobacco, kero and the stale fat from the chops.

Every day, Annie walks up the track to the road and waits for the Tremaines to come by in the truck.

Mr. Thompson is the schoolie. He believes in clean inkwells and no talking. He does not believe in shoes, not particularly.

Passionately, Mr. Thompson believes in his country. Each morning he has them sing "Advance Australia Fair": "We've golden soil and wealth for toil, Our home is dirt by sea."

"God Save the King" becomes "God Save the Queen." Mr. Thompson has them brush up on it before the inspector comes.

Mr. Thompson gets out the big map and tells stories of the explorers trying to find where the westward-flowing rivers went to. They got lost in the desert and died hungry, parched deaths.

After that Mr. Thompson talks about the fall of Singapore. It was the poms who gave it up; the Aussies would have fought and fought but no, the poms had to go and ruin it. Singapore wobbled and collapsed like plasticine.

One Aussie soldier died for every sleeper they laid on the Burma railway.

Mr. Thompson says this and then goes behind the black-board. What is he doing behind there?

"What's a sleeper?" Annie asks Uncle Reg.

Uncle Reg doesn't want to hear about the fall of Singapore. "Thommo shouldn't be telling youse kids," he says.

What Uncle Reg wants to hear about is the poetry. They sit out the back and Annie recites: "And at night the wondrous glory of the everlasting stars."

Uncle Reg sighs and hugs his chest with his arms.

In the evenings, when he doesn't have to go out fishing, Uncle Reg listens with Annie to "The Argonauts" on the radio. He listens carefully, with full seriousness—not like some adult pretending to be good. The Argonauts are Jason's band of happy rowers who are off to find the golden fleece. First on the Argonauts is the muddle-headed wombat, for the little ones. After that they read letters from kids who are real Argonauts. There is one Argonaut called Fido 12 who gets his letters read out all the time.

"It isn't fair," says Uncle Reg. "They should give the other kiddies a go."

After the Argonauts have finished, Uncle Reg gets the tea. He puts some fish in the frying pan. "We carved his name on a bloodwood tree," says Uncle Reg, pushing the fish around in the bacon fat, "With the date of his sad decease / And in place of 'Died from effects of spree' / We wrote, 'May he rest in peace.' "

After the fish and bread they have cups of tea. Then he brings out the can of Tongala condensed milk. Annie and Uncle Reg take turns dipping into the sweet, thick milk. It needs to be licked from the spoon. A nice big soup spoon. They pass the spoon back and forth.

Uncle Reg tests her out: "It was somewhere up the country, in a land of rock and scrub."

Annie knows this one. They both shout the next line: "That they formed an institution called the Geebung Polo Club."

On they go. It gets harder.

"The bishop sat in lordly state and purple cap sublime," Reg says.

Where is that from? "Wait a minute, wait a minute," Annie says, "I'm going to get it. Yes, I've got it, I've got it: 'On the outer Barcoo where the churches are few / And men of religion are scanty / On a road never cross'd 'cept by folk that are lost / One Michael Magee had a shanty.'"

"Nope, nope, nope," says Uncle Reg, in a quick, excited way.

This is serious stuff, they are really getting into it now. Alert, aroused, excited.

"The bishop sat in lordly state and purple cap sublime / And galvinised the old bush church at confirmation time." Uncle Reg is prompting. He wants to see her face when she realizes.

But no, she still can't place it.

"It's the day before the races," Uncle Reg goes on. He's giving it away, he's practically handing it to her on a plate.

"I've gone blank," she says. "Oh, help me, help me," she pleads.

He goes over to the butterbox in the alcove and brings out his treasures, his seven books: *Palgrave's Golden Treasury, Nine Miles from Gundagai, The Wide Brown Land, The Man from Snowy River, Around the Boree Log, Winnowed Verse, Bush Ballads and Galloping Rhymes.*

"Find it," he challenges.

In this way Annie learns about poetry from him, her Uncle Reg, her father's youngest brother.

The family came out from Cornwall. They gave the tin mining a go and then they took up sheep. But the sheep got crook. Coast disease.

Mr. Thompson tells them about coast disease. Not enough copper and cobalt in the soil. He writes the words on the board.

"What's cobalt?" Uncle Reg asks, when Annie provides this information.

Annie doesn't know.

"There's a cobalt blue in the paintbox," she suggests.

They try to puzzle things out.

On Saturday afternoons Uncle Reg fills an old milk urn with water and heats it up on the stove. Then he has a wash out the back. Clean and thirsty, he drives to town. Annie goes along for the ride; he drops her at the park while he goes to the pub.

The park is new. The Lions have cut back the tea tree, put in a tap and an old petrol drum for garbage. The park is for families who have begun to drive through town in their cars. The families have picnics in the sand. Mum screws the silver cup back on the thermos and says: "Where are the toilets? You'd think they'd have toilets." Dad and the kids go in the bushes. Mum doesn't go at all.

Annie lies on the ground and looks at the honeyeaters. Yellow and black, yellow mostly. They are standing on their heads to sip things from the banksia. Then she reads her book: *Biggles in the Baltic*.

When she gets sick of that she goes round to Aunty Marie's. At Aunty Marie's she can have a real bath, because Aunty Marie's got a proper bathtub and a chip bath heater.

But before she can light the chip bath heater, Annie has to sit on the back verandah and wait. Aunty Marie's having tea with some bloke.

Annie had a look in once. Aunty Marie was sitting on the posh sofa she had, drinking tea. The bloke was looking out the window. He didn't have anything on. His big wide brown back (I love a sunburnt country) and his white, white bum.

Annie knows about these things. The big girls at school have told her. Men want to get with women and take their clothes off. They make it sound like something loud and rude. They don't know anything. Aunty Marie and the bloke were as peaceful as the sand slithering on the dunes when the wind is down.

It's early winter. Uncle Reg is up before dawn, moving quietly, making a cuppa, putting the bacon on. He's going out for the mulloway.

At this time of year the mulloway are running up the inland shore. They're feeding on the softies — crabs that don't have their shell for a bit.

When breakfast is nearly ready, he gives his special whistle. That means that Annie must get up, because she is going with him.

Together they walk along the scrubby track, down to the water. Annie hops in the dinghy and sits on the fish box. Uncle Reg sits in front, in the middle thwart. Annie watches Uncle Reg's back as he rows (row Argonauts, row, row, row). Uncle Reg says you can smell when the fish are running, but Annie doesn't know what he's talking about.

The sand and the scrub recede. Annie can see long-legged birds with their yellow things hanging down on each side of their face (Mr. Thompson calls them wattles; but wattle is a bush). They make a high, complaining, anxious sound as they fly: they have lost something, they are afraid they won't find it. Then when they land it's a softer, deeper sound. They feel a bit better, though they're still worried.

Those are the plovers.

There are pelicans, too. Seaplanes, Uncle Reg says. He calls them Catalinas. The pelicans keep an eye on Uncle Reg and he keeps an eye on them: each knows that the other is after fish. The pelicans ride around the sky like heavy black and white boots, they are big and chunky and steady; they stick out their wings and hold up their enormous chests and Annie likes them. They come in to land by the bow of the boat, looking at Uncle Reg with grandfather eyes. Their little crew-cuts catch the wind, but they aren't silly; they're smart.

Uncle Reg tenses, waits. There it is. *Thwack chop* on the water. Mulloway, going after the mullet.

Uncle Reg really wants those big mulloway but only gets the mullet. Annie watches the mullet flopping about in the bottom of the boat, gasping for water, their golden irises staring. She waits carefully for the moment the thrashing fades into slackness.

A few minutes before they were sleek and silver and swift. And now this. She feels sticky.

With her bare feet and her unkempt clothes and drunken uncle, Annie provides opportunities for worry.

Aunty Marie, for one, worries.

Aunty Marie is a tall, fair, gloomy woman. She worries about the need to persist, to keep up, to care. Her scones are heavy, but she makes them over and over—for Annie, for Uncle Reg, for her blokes.

"She should be eating Oslo lunches," Aunty Marie says, to Uncle Reg.

"Oslo lunches?" Uncle Reg says, puzzled.

"Brown bread, cheese and lettuce, an apple," says Aunty Marie, pleased and relieved to have remembered, to have been for once so clear.

"You're always springing things on me," he grumbles.

"I only like white." Annie puts in.

Annie has the same thing for lunch every day. Uncle Reg makes them: two Vegemite sandwiches, two jam sandwiches. Nice white high-top loaf that comes with the mail once a week.

Next time they visit, Aunty Marie is almost in a good mood, almost brisk. With a definite swing of an arm, she opens the icebox and produces cheese, lettuce, apples. "Take them," she urges Uncle Reg. "You've got to give the kiddie a good foundation."

But such moments of resolve only lead to deeper waters.

"You should do something about her clothes," Aunty Marie tells Uncle Reg. "She's been running around like a little ragamuffin."

This is way beyond Uncle Reg. He's a man.

So Aunty Marie has a go, on her neighbour's sewing

machine. Frantic, pins in her mouth, she makes Annie try the frock on. Why oh why does the shoulder slump like that?

"Stand still," she snaps. "Stand still for heaven's sake."

She slaps Annie's leg.

The old aunts, Miss Brown and Miss Muriel Brown, also worry.

How can a girl go on like this, running wild and barefoot in the bush? The Misses decide that something must be done.

Miss Muriel's stern young man was more than one of the faces on the piano. He actually left her some money. It is this money, carefully guarded by the Commonwealth Bank, that is now dredged up to send Annie off to boarding school, there to enjoy the benefits of a convent school education.

When Annie was halfway through boarding school, Aunty Marie ran off to Adelaide with a bloke. Uncle Reg saw her walking down Rundle Street flashing a bloody great rock.

So far up herself, Uncle Reg said, she didn't even recognize me.

The worst times are when Uncle Reg comes to the school.

He does not come often. In his best clothes, looking shabby, he sits in the visitors' parlour, waiting for her.

Annie knows by now that he should be dead from shame.

But he sits there in the best convent chairs looking positively sure of himself, treating Reverend Mother with mock deference that is mostly gracious contempt and only a tiny bit fear.

Where on earth does he get the nerve? Annie wonders.

They drive down to one of the beaches. Uncle Reg has brought some old clothes from home, so Annie goes into the toilet and changes (carefully, though; the nuns have spies everywhere). The old clothes make her feel immensely better.

They buy fish and chips and sit on the sand.

Uncle Reg lies back. He doesn't have a towel, he just lets the sand get in his hair and everything. He puts his hat over his face.

"Gawd, I'm buggered," he says, cheerfully.

"When you came to see me, in the convent, you'd been out to the Port, hadn't you? Go on, admit it."

"Well, yes. You could say that," Reg says. "That'd be right."

He looks away from her, gives himself his slyest smile. Then his face closes down. After a while you run out of steam, he says.

This is a holiday morning, years later, when Annie is at university. Reg, she has discovered, is working class. He is someone you can brag about at parties. I mean, he's the real thing. That makes her the real thing, too, doesn't it? For there is by now another generation of stern young men, anti-this and anti-that, needing to be impressed.

At the Port, Uncle Reg would have done the round of a few watering holes, then picked himself up a prostitute. The unusual treat of sex gave him such confidence that even the convent parlour did not phase him.

"Did Reg drink at home?" Annie's current lover asks. "In the shack?"

Annie's current lover calls himself a feminist man (knows this is his only chance in life) and assures her that the world is full of men who rape and maim and pillage.

"Of course he drank at home," she replies. "He'd sit at the kitchen table and put away a bottle of plonk. Talkative at first, then later dead quiet. He'd move around the room with a heavy tread. Booze went straight to his feet. Sooner or later he'd do something clumsy, like knock the chair over. Then he'd swear, privately."

"Did he ever hit you?" her lover wants to know. He runs his fingers up and down her thighs.

"No, he never hit me. It never occurred to me that he might. Why would he hit *me*? I was what he had."

"Exactly the ones who get hit," Annie's lover says, closing his lips.

What does he want? Annie thinks. Doesn't he have enough already—a whole line of corpses lined up? No, he wants something more contemporary, less sentimental. Incest, child abuse, either or both. Or a more oblique devastation: love turned to indifference.

"At such times," she says, "Uncle Reg had that kind of sullen pathos that even now seems peculiarly male, peculiarly Australian."

Her lover smiles a little, at that. Her lover is an American himself. A social worker.

She does not tell him—she won't—that she lay in bed, shivering. Convinced Uncle Reg hadn't gone to town. He'd gone over the dunes. He'd walked right into the ocean in those big heavy boots and now he'd never be back.

"Uncle Reg would put on his slicker and go out into the night," she says. "He'd go into town. To Aunty Marie's."

"What you have to understand," Annie tells her lover, "is how different it was there. From here."

To the south the empty Southern ocean, winter storms coming in from the roaring forties. To the north, the desert, empty also, with summer messages of hot winds.

This is where the longest river in the country moves, dilatory, out to sea—lingering around lagoons and salt pans that are sometimes lakes, sometimes not. The soil cannot be farmed, and there is no one around.

The dunes go on, it seems, forever.

"When I was a child," she tells him, "you could walk for days among the dunes, beside that ocean, beside the lagoon. The birds in the sky would be all you would see."

She lifts her chin up and looks at her lover, accusingly.

They live in a northern city, where the skies are often low and pouty. They have a condominium. The ninth floor.

Annie cries out in her sleep.

Annie is out in the ocean and she's bobbing up and down. She's hanging on to a sleeper. Reg is on the other end.

Her lover doesn't call them sleepers. He calls them ties.

Family ties, he says.

Annie puts her head into her lover's neck. She can feel the vein in there, throbbing.

It is Christmas and they fly across the world, Annie and her lover, to be with Uncle Reg. She takes her lover to show him where she grew up (core of my heart, my country). He looks around at the lagoon, the dunes, the salt flats.

"You disappear into this," Annie tells him. "Like a lizard, like a crab."

"It's very flat out here, isn't it?" he says.

He looks up at the sky, and does not find it, so high and airy and distant it has become.

Annie leads him across the sand hills and shows him the black swans, feeding on the musk grass.

Some of the grass has been stranded in the heat.

"Phew, it stinks," he says.

"When the swans go after the tubers in the mud," Annie says, "you can hear them pulling them out — a marvellous, greedy, pulling sound. The tubers are rhizomes, actually. Do you know what rhizomes are?"

"No," he says. "But I suspect I'm about to find out."

"Out here," Annie says, "you can hear the blood climbing about your own body."

"Uh huh," he says.

"Listen," she commands. "Just listen."

They listen. But over the dunes, they hear a bunch of trail bikes coming. (Ridden by the gilded youths: their eyes are dull, their heads are flat, they have no brains at all.)

"I'd like to shoot them," Annie says. She imagines the motors sputtering a bit, then the silence. The silence would ripple outward, drift up into the sky. Within a week or two the sand would have covered them over. The ants would have gone to work.

"The sounds of the patriarchy are heard in the land," her lover says, virtuously.

Annie and her lover camp in a little tent beside the shack, a bright orange dome among the rocks. They have to get up early or get fried, it's so hot.

The shack is not what once it was. Reg has the electricity hooked up. On top of the wood stove—never used now—he has a TV. The antenna runs, handily, up the old chimney. Reg sits in front of the TV and lets it wash over him. He watches only the ABC, not out of snobbery, but because it's all he can get. With the same seriousness with which he used to listen to the Argonauts, Reg finds out about snooker, ballroom dancing, Solti in Budapest, nature.

"Do you know why it's called the right whale?" he asks.

"Yes, I do," says Annie.

"Because it was the right one for killing," he goes on.

"Disgusting," her lover says.

"Look at them scamper," he says, of the fox-trotting finalists. "Blooming rabbits."

"Yes," Annie agrees.

"I think that little one from Tassie's gunna win," Uncle Reg confides. "The one in the pink dress. No, not that one. That one."

Annie's lover goes for long walks along the dunes. She watches his back, diminishing; she sees him disappear into the mirage of summer.

They sit with Uncle Reg, out the back, waiting for the sun to go down. The lagoon, the dunes, the sky, are all leached white with the heat.

Her lover brings his recorder out and plays quietly, apologetically. The place is getting to him. Why should anyone want to know what his lungs, his tongue, his throat, his fingers, his heart, are doing? What does it matter?

Annie puts her feet up on a pile of old rope. She should move back here, chuck it all in. They could live on fish. Just her and Reg.

She should be with him. It isn't right, being so far away.

Reg is in a gloomy mood. He doesn't drink these days. Instead, he takes little pills for his heart and announces he's not long for this world. His books of poetry are kept now — Annie is displeased to note — in a bookshelf. He still recites, but he tends towards the maudlin.

He says: "When we sat in the sunlight, Annie / I dreamt that the skies were blue."

"Come off it, Reg," says Annie.

He says nothing.

"It's the day before the races," she says, to Reg, to cheer herself up.

"Out at Tangmalangaloo," Reg shoots back, automatically.

"Sharp as a tack, you old coot," Annie says, pleased.

"How does it go?" Uncle Reg asks. Willing to make the effort, willing to get into it.

" 'Come tell me boy,' His Lordship said, in crushing tones severe," she offers, happy she can remember. " 'Come tell me, why is Christmas Day the greatest of the year?' "

Yes, it's going to work. This has always worked between them.

"A squall of knowledge hit the lad from Tangmalangaloo," says Uncle Reg. And how the words are smooth and sure now, how like whiskey, really. "He gave a lurch which set ashake the vases on the shelf, / He knocked the benches all askew, upending of himself."

Reg pauses; he's passing the lines back to Annie, who knows.

Annie says: "And oh, how pleased His Lordship was, and how he smiled to say, / 'That's good, my boy. Come tell me now; and what is Christmas Day?' "

She stops. Uncle Reg is to have the punch lines, it's fitting.

He says: "The ready answer bared a fact no bishop ever knew — / 'It's the day before the races out at Tangmalangaloo.' "

So it goes, between them, the old-fashioned poetry, their code world: sentimental, mediocre, garbage really, all but forgotten; but exclusive, triumphalist, familiar; theirs.

Moira

SUSANNA held Moira's hand at parties and introduced her, saying, "I want you to meet Moira. Moira is taking the Church of Rome apart brick by brick."

(This was in New Haven, in the sixties. Moira was doing her doctorate; she was writing her thesis on Auden.)

Moira, hearing Susanna's introduction, would see in her mind the bricks of the convent school she had attended back home and the bricks of the big cathedral beside it. Together, the convent and cathedral took up an entire town block.

And Moira would be daunted by the task ahead.

While building the cathedral tower a man had fallen to his death. He had gone straight to heaven, the nuns said, because his work was an act of faith.

⁂

When I became part of Moira's care team I signed up for early mornings.

Early mornings are her best time, Inez says.

We sit in the garden, in the sunshine. The garden is at the back of her home in North Sydney, the home she shares with her lover, Inez.

Moira has her cushions, she has her hat. I bring her pills, something to drink.

We have three garden chairs: one for her, one for me and one for her massive tabby tomcat, Mad Max.

Moira needs her painkillers every four hours. But at the top of that time, in hours one and two, she's relaxed.

The wattle is out, a nervy gold-and-black shivering behind the garage.

"Good job we're not allergic," Moira says. "You and me."

She touches my arm.

There's something perhaps I should mention: if I become aware of myself, standing in the supermarket in front of the grapefruit, let's say, I am puzzled to find myself there.

I am picking out fruit, and I know this must be part of a plan: put the grapefruit into the bag, take them to the checkout, carry them home. Eat them.

So that when Moira touches me, I am taken by surprise.

Moira's my boss. Was my boss. We teach English at the TAFE, the College of Technical and Further Education; she's the department head.

We're allies at work. Have been for years.

Soon after the diagnosis, she was still feeling quite well, still coming in to work, cracking jokes, chairing meetings.

"I just don't want to be shunted off to a hospital room," she said. "Some daggy little broom closet."

The alternative, she knew, would mean having people available around the clock.

"I'll have to go out into the highways and hedgerows and compel them to come in," she said, laughing.

"Bring in hither the poor, and the maimed, and the halt, and the blind," I said.

She asked me if I wanted to be part of her care team when the time came.

"You do wonder," she said, "what's going to happen next."

We sit in the garden and Moira tells me stories. How she went back to the town where she grew up and found that the school had been closed down.

"The bricks were all still there but the nuns had gone," Moira says.

In her garden the red-whiskered bulbuls are singing. We listen to their jaunty, falling whistle.

She'd lost touch with Susanna.

The last time Moira saw Susanna, Susanna was living in upstate New York with a woman who had three full-sized poodles. This woman, who was a therapist in demand, left the housework and the dogs to Susanna.

"I always knew she'd make a mess of things," Moira says.

I imagine Susanna. She is being hustled across a park by large excited dogs. She has their leashes in a tangle.

"Susanna was the love of my life," Moira adds. "It was quite a long time ago."

They were both teaching assistants, Moira and Susanna. That was how they met.

"I was just terrible," Moira says. "I'd have the students sit round in a circle and I'd stare at them and ask, What do you think the poet means when he says, *We must love one another or die?*"

When my mother was in hospital, I was in Sydney and she was in Adelaide. I could not get away.

My son was an infant in my arms.

I did go down to see Mum, but only twice. "Couldn't take the time, I see," Mum said. "Too busy with your own concerns."

I don't know what painkillers they gave them then, but whatever they were, they weren't enough.

Those of us who are on Moira's care team had an initial meeting at her house. Convened by Inez. The front room was crowded—about twenty people. Women, mostly. The neighbours from both sides: the Chowdhrys and old Mrs. Morrison.

Moira was there, in the best chair. And Inez, of course, bossing us around: sit here, sit there, bring another chair from the kitchen.

Inez has that frizzy hair that sticks out all round.

I know what slot I fall into: From the TAFE. Straight.

Inez made us have a round of sorts, to say who we were and why we thought we wanted to do this.

"It will take a lot of emotional energy," Inez said. "It's a big commitment."

As if we didn't know that.

I explained about my mother.

Mrs. Chowdhry said, in an emphatic, clear voice: "We want to help because it's Moira." Mr. Chowdhry and the two embarrassed big sons nodded.

Mrs. Morrison said, simply, "We love you, Moira."

Inez looked a bit pissed off at that. As if she wanted dibs on all of the loving herself.

It is in fiction that I meet women I understand. They are floating on the ceiling or drifting about the sky while the weather passes through them.

In the real world, however, things are not like this. There is talk instead of self-esteem, high and low.

A crowd scene in a sauna: some of the women have thighs that make a tiny sucking sound as they get up from the bench and run, with gleaming breasts, into the cold showers. Those are the ones who have high self-esteem.

Long before she met Susanna, when she was a young woman of twenty-two, Moira was engaged.

At that time Moira worked in the library in Armidale, in northern New South Wales. The library had been built in honour of those who had been killed in World War II.

Each workday morning Moira left her flat and rode her bike down the hill to work. She picked up the books that had tumbled through the after-hours slot. Then she turned a page in the book of remembrance. The book sat in the foyer on a little podium, inside a glass case.

Once in a while she would turn to the page that had her father's name on it.

Captain John Halverson, Tarakan, 1945.

"Where the hell is Tarakan?" I ask Inez.

"Telling you that story, is she?" says Inez.

Someone from the night shift has left cheese on a plate by the sink, attracting a multitude of small brown ants.

Inez runs the tap and washes the ants down.

Now I know for a fact that Moira would never do a thing like that. When ants walked all over the sink at work Moira would knock her knuckles on the counter, address them: "Come along, chaps. Time, gentlemen, time."

She'd wait until the ants had hurried off through their crack in the tiles.

"What sort of a night did she have?" I ask Inez.

"Not so good," Inez says.

Moira and Inez have been together for nine years. They'd been going to break up, before the diagnosis. Then they renegotiated.

"She has someone else," Moira says.

Moira pulls her hat down over her face.

"You do know that, don't you?" Moira adds.

I live with my son. I haven't had anyone since — as my own mother would have put it — Bully was a pup.

I am one of those women couples speculate about.

What does she do?

Probably perfectly happy on her own.

Probably.

Moira tells me about her mother. Moira's mother fell in love with a Methodist, a shocking thing.

Her parents disapproved. They beseeched, they prayed.

His parents went one better — disowned him completely.

They were married, Moira's mother and the disowned Methodist, in the Catholic church registry. No nuptial mass, no nuptial blessing, no flowers, no wedding music.

"In hugger-mugger," Moira says. "Such a begrudged, half-hearted ceremony."

But in the snaps of the wedding her mother and father look — despite his uniform and her street clothes — ecstatic, triumphant. (This in an era when, in the face of the wedding photographer, restraint was customary.)

Moira sent me into her study to find the album for her. She showed me these pictures, proof.

After her father was killed by a sniper at Tarakan in Borneo, Moira tells me, her mother gave up.

"She signed off," Moira says.

Her mother took a job cooking and cleaning at the local Catholic boys' school where her brother was a Brother.

"There was no need for her to bury herself like that," says Moira.

"You mustn't do that," she adds. "You mustn't give up."

Moira's theory: Her mother, having had a brief period of defiant physical love, felt deeply punished, rebuked, by her husband's death.

Moira's mother went daily to mass in the boys' school chapel. It had a side alcove built especially for the maids. The alcove faced the altar at right angles, so that the boys couldn't see them, the women.

"She had my father's picture on the dressing table," Moira says. "In his army uniform. With his hat band riding on his chin."

Having said that, Moira, without warning, begins to weep.

It happens. She'll be going along, telling me her stories, doing fine, and then it's as if she has stepped on a trap door, fallen through.

At such times, I take her hand. "Moira," I say, "Moira. It's all right, Moira." Although it isn't.

Young Moira rode her bike to St. Angela's, away on the other side of town.

Her mother's piety was well-known to the nuns, and her father's unfortunate religion had been cancelled out by the happy certainty of his death. Moira had no difficulty getting someone to walk beside her when they were being marched in a crocodile over to the cathedral, which was often.

But in high school Moira developed a crush on the baddest of the Bad Girls.

Bad Girls came from Sydney. They were sent away to the country, to boarding school, to get straightened out.

This Bad Girl had hung around milk bars with bodgies, gone for rides on their motor bikes. She wore a medallion around her neck, not of the Virgin Mary but of James Dean. She chewed gum and giggled during the rosary.

Sometimes Bad Girl stood by the coal shed, waiting for Moira. They would go inside and smooch. "Or whatever we called it then," Moira says.

"I got less daring as time went on," she says.

"But I shouldn't be talking all the time," Moira says. "Tell me about yourself."

Of course, there is Martin.

My son, Martin, is eighteen.

Martin sits in his room and listens to jazz on winter Sunday afternoons. In this music, the fog rolls in from the ocean and you admit that, for you, it's not likely to happen ever again— the passion, the overwhelming happiness.

"An eighteen-year-old shouldn't be tuned in to that," I tell Moira.

"Maybe he doesn't hear what you do," she says. "Maybe he hears something quite different."

"What about lovers?" Moira asks.

I was afraid she would.

The palliative care nurses come.

One of them talks non-stop about pain management, then says, "My husband has lupus. Unfortunately."

Another dips her head and blushes at the posters on the bedroom wall.

The third smiles too much. "What do you bet she takes a swig of that liquid morphine before she comes in," Moira says.

They keep a logbook about what they call TLCs.

"Doesn't it just make you want to throw up?" Moira says.

Moira, an undergraduate at university, went to the Newman Society barbecue and got herself a boyfriend.

"Charred chops and endless beer," she says.

"Dreadful drinking songs," I add.

We sing them, the bits we can remember: "Oh, I do want to be a Roman Catholic / Oh, I do want to join the Church of Rome / Oh, I do want to be a lackey of the priests / And get as drunk as blazes on the major feasts."

We're really getting into this when Inez comes striding across the lawn, to say bye-bye, she's off to work.

Inez is often jumping into her car and driving away. Inez is a lawyer; she specializes in international law. She has a new lover, in Germany. They get together when Inez is in Brussels or at The Hague.

"Her name is Inge," Moira tells me.

"Inez and Inge," I say.

It sounds like a porn movie, but I don't say that. I suppose it's none of my business, even though she's talking to me about it.

We both watch the car pull out of the driveway; a quick toot of the horn, and off down the street.

I tell Moira what I read in the papers.

They did this survey about being in love. Ten per cent said they had never been in love. Ten per cent said they had been in love but had found it too painful.

Moira lies back on the cushions and I brush her hair. Her hair is thick, salt and black pepper. Irish hair.

I look down at her face, at the lines around her eyes.

She's losing a lot of weight and her body is smaller, more bony.

The doctors are cagey.

She could go on for years, they say. You never know.

The others in the care team will have to go back to their work, their families, their own lives.

I will stay on, combing Moira's hair in the garden.

"Love is so terribly important," I tell Martin. "All kinds. You have to be willing to take risks, to go for it."

Martin looks at me, briefly wary.

"If you don't you'll regret it later," I say.

Martin is sitting at the breakfast table, eating. His silky young skin stretches over growing bones; daily, he is more fresh, more handsome, more like his father must have been at his age.

"Does she look any different, Mum?" Martin asks.

"No, love," I say. To reassure.

But Moira makes terrible, out-of-fashion jokes. "Eat your heart out, Bobby Sands," she says.

This is how it will be: I am strolling on a beach with her.

We have walked down through the tough, delicate bush, moving quietly, aware of small eyes taking note.

Her arm is in mine because she is still weak. What a break, she says—leaning on me—what luck, what a bonus, what a marvellous encore.

Inez will be off on one of her trips.

So Moira had this boyfriend named Michael. The son of a doctor. Who sat beside her on the bus during Newman Society outings. Kissed her, she claims, during the singing of "Michael, Row the Boat Ashore."

"All very wet," Moira says.

He wanted to marry her, did Michael.

I'll take him home to my mother, decided Moira. And that will be that.

Her mother, slouching around with the other school maids on Sunday afternoons. Her mother, in her wool socks, drinking tea and looking at magazines.

For afternoon tea, her mother made up some pink icing and stuck it between wholemeal biscuits.

On the washing line, the maids' underwear flapped, large and dangerous and far too real.

They sat on packing cases in the sun and studied the floor plans in *House and Gardens*. "Look at this," her mother said, "it isn't fair. Master bedroom, master bedroom. Why should the son always get the biggest room?"

But that wasn't that. The doctor's son went ahead and bought the engagement ring anyway.

Moira wore it to her part-time job in the library.

The Anglican bishop, who had come in for his weekly supply of westerns, admired it.

Moira, in a wide fifties skirt, twin set and Peter Pan collar, holding out her engagement ring finger to the bishop.

"Three guesses what I did," Moira says.

"Don't need them," I say, pleased with myself.

He was a lecturer at the university, from England.

He came to the library and sat in the periodicals section and stared at Moira when she took the books off the trolley and reached up to put them in the shelves.

It was a seduction based entirely on words, says Moira. She sends me into her study in search of the book, claims to be able to find the exact passage.

"Here it is," she says, and reads: " '. . . she received the maximum of unspeakable communication in touch, dark, subtle, positively silent, a magnificent gift and give again, a perfect acceptance and yielding, a mystery, the reality of that which can never be known, vital, sensual reality that can never be transmuted into mind content, but remains outside, living body of darkness and silence and subtlety, the mystic body of reality. She had her desire fulfilled.' "

Moira laughs. She rereads the last sentence.

I don't know if I should laugh or not.

I don't feel like laughing.

I reach right back and tell Moira about Martin's father, how he left me when I began to show with Martin.

"Perhaps he was the love of my life," I say.

I tell her about another man, from, well, quite a few years ago.

His interminable marriage.

Inez is furious. She paces up and down the kitchen and cannot calm down.

"Who the fuck helped themselves to Moira's tarts?" she yells.

Someone on the night shift has eaten them.

Jam tarts are the only food that attracts Moira these days. (Mostly she just drinks Sustagen; she has trouble keeping things down.)

Inez buys these tarts in a cakeshop in the Strand Arcade. She calls them linzertorte.

"What creature would do a thing like that?" demands Inez. "This bloody well takes the cake," she says, unaware.

Moira, in the living room on cushions, laughs. Rings her bell.

Someone on the team has given her a little brass bell so that she can let us know if she needs us, if we happen to be out of the room.

"Did some knave stole those tarts all away?" Moira asks. (She's in good form this morning.)

Inez bursts into tears.

"Come here, my little jam tart," Moira says to Inez.

Inez puts her face into Moira's neck and they murmur together.

Inez begins to lick Moira's ear.

We've finished with the doctor's son and the university lecturer.

At last, we are up to Susanna.

But before she can tell me all about Susanna, Moira has a setback.

I arrive for my morning shift and Inez stands in the doorway, her arms hanging down, hands slack.

Last night Moira was in a sort of coma.

"We thought this might be it," Inez says.

Moira isn't the same after that.

Her energy is down; she doesn't want to go out into the garden in the morning any more.

Instead of talking with Moira, I do the washing.

Moira now has prodigious night sweats. The sheets and her nightgown have to be changed three or four times each night.

When I go in and out of her room, Moira smiles at me but in an unfocussed, polite way.

As if I were some stranger.

One morning I go in to see her and she gestures to me to come close. (Inez is in the living room, talking on the phone.) Moira reaches up and takes both my hands.

"I want you to do something for me," she whispers. "I need you to get in touch with Susanna."

She lies back on the cushions. Forces herself to go on.

"Tell Susanna I have to see her," she urges. "Find her. Make her come."

I wait until Inez goes out to work so I can search through Moira's study for her old address books. Eventually I find Susanna's name, and a bunch of crossed-out addresses.

I take all the address books home and carry them into the house as if they were fragile, contraband.

I dial the numbers, overseas, to the States, to Canada.

People with strange accents come on the line and can't understand what I'm saying.

I have to repeat myself.

You must have the wrong number.

No, sorry.

Lady, are you a nut or what? Like I told you before. She ain't here, period.

After work, I go into the city to the GPO and look in all the phone books. I call the library and talk to the reference librarian.

I call information for the major cities on the northeast coast of the United States, of Canada. Then I call the numbers.

I make a list of the names of these cities. There are 287 cities on my list.

Piece by piece by piece, I am going to solve this puzzle. I am going to find Susanna.

I will find Susanna for you.

I will bring her to you.

I whisper into the bathroom mirror, making it fog over.

One day there is a new roster on the refrigerator and my name isn't on it. There must be some mistake.

Right away I go into the bedroom, but Moira is curled up under the quilt, asleep. In the crook of her legs, Mad Max is licking his bum.

So I ask the woman who's going off shift. Like me, she's from the TAFE; straight. I know her quite well.

She says, "They're going to move Moira's bed into the living room. Put their mattresses down so they can sleep around her, like a laager. That way, if someone who's watching her needs help, with moving her or something, they'll be right there."

"So what's this list for?" I ask

"It's the list for sleeping over."

"Why aren't I on the list for sleeping over?"

She looks at me in a shrewd way.

"I could do it, Martin's old enough," I protest.

She says, "Well, who would you want around? Wouldn't you want your old lovers? They're the ones I'd want, for sure."

She laughs.

"Old lovers," I say, as if I do not understand.

This woman has been married to her husband forever. Every time I see him he has his head behind a newspaper. The sports section.

What could she possibly know about old lovers?

But it was me Moira asked to find Susanna.

I think constantly of Susanna. Where is she? What is she doing right now?

Susanna is walking along a city street, or eating a piece of bread, or opening a window.

(Behind her, in an unkempt apartment, the phone rings and rings.)

Susanna, not thinking of Moira.

Her head full of her own life, somewhere.

"What are you up to, Mum?" Martin asks.

He used to call me by my name when he was younger. Now he calls me Mum.

I'm cleaning out the spare room. For Susanna. Vacuuming, dusting, airing the room, putting out potpourri in a dark blue bowl. My cheeks are warm, my hands supple.

"She's coming," I tell him. "That friend of Moira's."

"But Mum," he says.

"But Mum nothing," I say. "She's coming."

Martin is helping me. We sit at the dining-room table, going through the lists.

"That just about wraps up Massachusetts, Mum," Martin says.

When Susanna comes, she will see how Martin is. How casual and generous in his young beauty.

Susanna will be the right age to appreciate Martin, my son.

I think I may have found her number. It was amazing luck, I was down to the sixty-seventh city on the list. I dialled this number in Toronto and there was a taped answer.

The voice sounded exactly right.

I left a message for her to call me as soon as possible.

She's the one.

I believe she's the one. I really believe that.

She'll come right away. I'll meet her at the airport, bring her to Moira.

For a break—because she'll need a break—I'll take her up to Dee Why and she can be impressed by the waves and sand. And the beach will have the clarity of very early spring, before the sun washes everything out.

For light relief I'll explain to Susanna about the battle for the beaches. (What do we want? No more pooh! When do we want it? Now!)

She will know that Moira and I have a special connection; I won't need to explain.

But I'll tell her when she asks. About Moira's comfort with me, her frankness.

We will walk along the beach, Susanna and I, and we'll both be thinking about that.

"Inez," I say, pleased to have caught her in time. "I've got to talk to you." For once with Inez I feel confident, in charge. We are standing in the driveway. (Ms Lawyer is off to the city, again.)

"It's about Susanna."

As I say this, Inez looks, briefly, as if she is falling through space.

Then she pulls herself together.

"Don't tell me," she says, intensely irritated. "Not you too."

I stare at her.

"I suppose Moira's been asking you to help her find Susanna."

Has she been eavesdropping?

Does she know I went through Moira's things in her study?

"She's asked us," says Inez, slowly, emphatically. "All of us. Ages ago."

I don't believe it.

"We've tried and tried. We've been driving Telecom crazy. But we've had to face it, we just can't find her."

"I guess you were her last resort," she says.

Then she started to laugh.

She turned around and walked back into the house. Went to the kitchen, where the night shift, the sleep-overs, were making breakfast.

I go out to the laundry. Take out a load of washing someone has left there. Put in a new load.

Measure the laundry soap, set the dial, make the wash turn and tumble. See, I am quite capable of doing these things.

Take out Moira's sheets and the T-shirts she wears as nighties.

Hang them on the line where the sun shines, as it has to.

Out on the street, people are walking along. They are going to catch the train to work.

She would have told the others her stories, too. All of them.

Ages ago. Different bits for different people.

For me, early life, religion and men. Auden, Lawrence.

From where I am, I can hear them.

Someone has just quipped "desperately seeking Susanna," and they all laugh.

It's laughter that says, this is totally crazy; this is serious.

It's laughter that says, we're deep into it here, my friends. And if it's a miracle you're waiting for, well, don't count on it, matey, but one might show up, you never know, it just might.

You hear a lot of this laughter around Moira's house these days.

Listen to it, coming from the kitchen, now.